CORGI CASE FILES

CASE OF THE

STUTTERING
PARROT

J.M. POOLE

Mysteries by J.M. Poole
The Corgi Case Files Series
Available in e-book and paperback

Case of the One-Eyed Tiger
Case of the Fleet-Footed Mummy
Case of the Holiday Hijinks
Case of the Pilfered Pooches
Case of the Muffin Murders
Case of the Chatty Roadrunner
Case of the Highland House Haunting
Case of the Ostentatious Otters
Case of the Dysfunctional Daredevils
Case of the Abandoned Bones
Case of the Great Cranberry Caper
Case of the Shady Shamrock
Case of the Ragin' Cajun
Case of the Missing Marine
Case of the Stuttering Parrot

If you enjoy Epic Fantasy,
check out Jeff's other series:
Pirates of Perz
Tales of Lentari
Bakkian Chronicles

CORGI CASE FILES

CASE OF THE

STUTTERING
PARROT

BOOK 15

J.M. POOLE

Secret Staircase Books

Case of the Stuttering Parrot
Published by Secret Staircase Books, an imprint of
Columbine Publishing Group, LLC
PO Box 416, Angel Fire, NM 87710

Book layout and design by Secret Staircase Books
Cover image by Felipe de Barros

First trade paperback edition: March, 2022

First e-book edition: March, 2022

* * *

Publisher's Cataloging-in-Publication Data

Poole, J.M.
Case of the Stuttering Parrot / by J.M. Poole.
p. cm.
ISBN 978-1649140807 (paperback)
ISBN 978-1649140814 (e-book)

1. Zachary Anderson (Fictitious character)—Fiction. 2. Amateur
sleuth—Fiction. 3. Pomme Valley, Oregon (Fictitious location)—
Fiction. 4. Pet detectives—Fiction. I. Title

Corgi Case Files Mystery Series : Book 15.
Poole, J.M., Corgi Case Files mysteries.

BISAC : FICTION / Mystery & Detective.

813/.54

For my father, James William Poole (1946-2021)

Life took you too soon. I hope — wherever you are — you're at peace and have reunited with your beloved pups.

Acknowledgements

One of the things I'm told over and over is that the readers seem to enjoy the progression of events in PV: Zack's relationship, expansion at the winery, and so on. For this book, I'm introducing another expansion, and that'll be the living arrangements. So, with that in mind, I'd like to thank my wife, Giliane, for stepping up to the plate and choosing a set of plans for Zack and Jillian's ... nope, no spoilers here. When you get to the part I'm talking about, you'll know that the person who chose that particular set of plans was my wife.

I'd also like to extend a big thank you for everyone who beta read for me. Members of my Posse for this time around was: Jason, Michelle, Elizabeth, Carol, Caryl, Diane, and Louise. I would also like to thank my team of readers at Secret Staircase Books: Marcia, Susan, Sandra, and Paula.

As I've mentioned before, the locations in this story are based on real-life cities and towns in southwestern Oregon. I've taken liberties with certain areas, streets, and buildings, so if you happen to live in this area and see that I've completely moved roads to suit my intentions, renamed buildings, and so on, please, no hate mail. :)

Finally, I'd like to thank you, the reader, for allowing me to continue the adventures in Pomme Valley with two feisty corgis. It's a dream come true.

J.

ONE

"Did I hear you right? You didn't just say what I think you said, did you?"

The couple, a man in his mid-forties and a woman in her late thirties, were walking—hand-in-hand—through row after row of healthy green plants. Each of these plants, it should be noted, was growing on its own dedicated trellis. Also worth noting was how each plant was equidistant from its neighbors, and the rows they comprised were straight-as-an-arrow and looked so perfect that passing observers could easily imagine some type of machine overseeing everything.

The man, six feet tall, with graying brown hair and a

medium build, pulled his companion to a stop and wrapped his arms around her. The woman, shorter than him by at least half a foot, flipped her long brown locks out of her face before returning the hug.

"I meant it. Every word. I want you to be happy. I know you've been wanting this for a while now."

"And you haven't?" the woman returned.

"If we're being honest, then yes, I guess I have."

"You don't sound that convincing, Zachary."

"It's a big decision, Jillian. It'll mean a lot of money, hard work, and …"

"… headaches?" Jillian finished for me.

"Well, yeah, there's that."

We reached the end of this particular field and just like that, the vines fell away, only to be replaced by practically every berry bush you could think of, and then some. Stopping long enough to pluck a couple of fat ripe blackberries from a passing bush, I handed one to Jillian while tossing mine up in the air and catching it with my mouth.

"That could have ended badly," Jillian laughed. "Then again, that might explain some of the stains I've been finding on your shirts."

"My aim isn't that far off," I complained. "Now, you were saying?"

"Right. Issues. Okay, you mentioned the topic of money."

I nodded. "That's an important one."

"Well, we're both successful business owners. We have more than enough in the bank to cover any expense which may arise."

"True, but I don't think you have any idea just how

expensive this is gonna be," I argued. "We're talking thousands of dollars here, my dear. Hundreds of thousands."

Jillian shrugged. "So, what else are we going to do with the money? Now, next up, we have the hard work you mentioned. Well, of course, it'll be hard."

"And inconvenient, too," I added.

"Something like this will never be convenient. But, I think with a lot of patience, and hard work on both of our parts, we can make it happen."

"What about the headache bit?" I asked, giving my companion a smile. "I don't think there is anything we can do about that."

"Sure there is," my wife countered. "That's what ibuprofen is for."

I had to laugh. She had me there. Still, as I gazed out at the open acreage of Lentari Cellars, I had to shake my head. I have grown very comfortable with my life here, in Southwestern Oregon. Now, what I was proposing to do was going to throw everything in turmoil. Having never been one who was good with change, I had to ask myself: was this what I really wanted to do?

Before I go too much farther, I probably should introduce myself. After all, I don't want to lose you right off the bat. Now, my name is Zachary Anderson, but you can call me Zack. Everyone does. Well, most everyone. My mother, living in Phoenix, Arizona, and my new wife, Jillian, seem to be the only two who ever address me as Zachary. As for me, I'm in my mid-forties. I'd like to say that I'm fairly fit, but let's face it. Everyone tends to smudge the facts just a bit when asked to describe their physical fitness. I work out (when the mood arises) regularly, and always seem to be chasing my two dogs.

My wife, Jillian, is in her late thirties. She owns and operates a local business in town called Cookbook Nook. It's a specialty kitchen store offering cookbooks, cooking-based knickknacks that most people didn't realize they needed, and tasty morsels offered in a small café on the second floor. Jillian keeps herself in good shape simply by working at her store. Having spent an inordinate amount of time at my wife's place of business, I can attest to the strenuous physical activity necessary to keep that place running smoothly.

One would think a specialty store like hers, in a tiny town like Pomme Valley, wouldn't be a good match, only they'd be wrong. Jillian's store has to be one of the busiest in Pomme Valley, and as such, she is always on the go. Fill this order, grab that from the back, go upstairs to deal with a problem in the café, or run to Gary's Grocery to replace some missing ingredients: it's all in a day's work. The poor woman never stops moving!

As much as I'd like to suggest putting a step-counter on her, just for curiosity's sake, I won't. I know full well that Jillian would want to put one on me as well, and then we'd have the makings of a competition. Seeing as how I spend the majority of my day in a chair outfitted with wheels, I can tell you that my numbers would pale in comparison to hers.

Speaking of my wife, here's something you probably don't know. As far as Pomme Valley's citizens are concerned, she is their guardian angel, their Secret Santa, and would be called Ms. Moneybags if they knew how much she donated to the city.

Let me explain.

Jillian's first husband, a wickedly savvy businessman by the name of Michael, made an absolute ton of money, doing who-knows-what. Sadly, the poor fellow passed away from cancer, and left everything to his widow. Now, seeing how I never share the financial details about my new wife with anyone, let's just say that Jillian is the modern day equivalent of Richie Rich. If you don't know who that is, I suggest you look it up. I consider myself very financially stable, but compared to Jillian, once again the numbers pale in comparison.

Thankfully, it's something that has never bothered me. Jillian is free to do whatever she wants with her money. That brings us back around to the guardian angel bit I mentioned earlier. Jillian has taken it upon herself to help her friends open the businesses of their dreams. Bakery? Florist? Realtor? You name the company, and Jillian is probably the silent partner. But ... does she lord this over her friends? Will she ever step in and override anyone's orders? Nope. Not once have I ever seen her exert her influence over anyone, aside from an occasional nod or look at one of the employees.

We are a good couple. They say that opposites attract. Well, in our case, it's true. Jillian is extroverted and very outgoing. She enjoys large groups of people and can effortlessly mingle with anyone, from sharing a joke with the janitor sweeping the floors to having tea with PV's mayor.

As for me? Well, I'm more introverted. We writers tend to enjoy quiet time alone. I'm happiest in front of my keyboard, laying out complex romance plots, figuring out how to get two characters together who absolutely hate each other, and ...

WOOF!

Oh, yes. I can't forget *them*. There are two others in my house that need introductions. Down there, rising no higher than my knees—unless they rear up on their squat hind legs—are a pair of corgis. Pembroke Welsh Corgis, if you'd like to get technical. I can honestly say that I wasn't a dog owner when I first moved to Oregon. But, less than twenty-four hours later, I had been talked into adopting a canine companion by my best friend from high school, Harry Watt.

Dr. Harrison Watt, PV's veterinarian, just so happened to settle down in the same small Oregon town as me. My old friend was married, had two kids, and—this still freaks me out—is an actual doctor. If you had known Harry in his younger years, you'd know why I found that so hard to believe. Anyway, Harry pretty much forced Sherlock, my first dog, on me and didn't allow me to say no. In retrospect, I'm very thankful he didn't. That furry little booger has changed my life and I can't imagine a day going by without having him by my side. Maybe it's because that little corgi has an innate ability to solve mysteries?

I kid you not.

Sherlock, just like his namesake, can locate clues so obscure you'd think he was looking at random things. However, once they were applied to the case I was working on, then you'd be able to …

I'm getting ahead of myself. Sorry 'bout that. Let me backstep a bit.

In addition to being a writer, I'm also a paid police consultant for the local Pomme Valley police. Do I possess any skills that qualify me for the job? Not a one. As long as we're being honest, let me get something off my chest:

the only thing the police department is interested in is my dogs' opinions. Sherlock and Watson are … wow, I'm not any good at this, am I? Some writer I am. I'm jumping ahead of myself yet again.

After I first moved to town and adopted Sherlock, I was accused of murder. I won't go into details, since it's a story I've already told, but Sherlock was pretty much responsible for keeping my tail out of the slammer. Somehow, and I've yet to figure out how, that little dog sniffed out clues that were related to the case. It might not be clear at the time of discovery, so I got into the habit of snapping pictures of whatever catches the dogs' attention. Therefore, if you ever hear me mention something called *corgi clues*, then you'll know what I'm talking about.

Anyway, after Sherlock managed to solve the case, and the charges against me were dropped, I bumped into Harry and voila! I had a second corgi. This one was a timid red and white female. Now, I know you'll laugh, especially knowing she's a girl, but I named her Watson. Sherlock and Watson. What can I say? I think it's cute.

As I was saying, in addition to being a writer, I'm also a police consultant. Thankfully, our small town doesn't see too much crime. Then again, for a time, everyone thought I had brought the crime with me from Arizona, seeing as how we've had murders, burglaries, and all manner of crime befall us and that was *after* I had moved to town. Vance, the detective who had originally arrested me for murder, became good friends with me and, to this day, still heckles me about the blissful days of BZ.

Jerk.

That was in the past. Today, it's all I can do to keep myself from daydreaming about the future. After all, after losing my first wife to a terrible car crash a few years ago, I never thought I'd see myself married again. Now, on the other hand, I don't think I've ever been happier, and I would have bet any amount of money that, prior to moving to Oregon, no one would ever have heard me utter those words again.

On this particular day, Jillian and I were walking through the vineyards of Lentari Cellars. Caden, my winemaster, had been encouraging me to learn more about the fine art of wine-making. The problem was, I hated the stuff, and he knew it. I swear he was doing everything in his power to expose me more and more to the process, hoping that I'll somehow become more tolerant of the nasty liquid. It's no secret that I do not hide my disdain of wine. Red, white, grape, berry, it really didn't matter. No matter how hard I tried, I could not bring myself to take the tiniest of sips.

There are exceptions, of course. A while back, Caden came up with a super-limited dessert wine, made from some I-kid-you-not *moldy* grapes. Oh, he assured me it was the good kind of mold, but then again, I didn't even know there was such a thing *as* good mold. That particular recipe, as Caden calls it, was surprisingly sweet and did not have any of the after-effects I detested from trying other wines. So, come fall each year, Caden dedicates a small chunk of acreage for the exact purpose of creating moldy grapes. His method doesn't always work, but so far, he's had moderate success.

There was a final way that I could say I enjoyed the smell—and taste—of wine. Red wine, to be specific. That was when the holidays came around. Jillian has a way of cooking her turkeys with red wine, and for once, I didn't find myself cringing from the smell. Apparently, if I knew the wine was being served over a nice, golden-brown bird, then I was okay with it. Oh, don't get me wrong. I'm sure the simple fact that the alcohol was baked right out of the wine had something to do with it.

Back to the present, Sherlock and Watson were playing a noisy game of tag. One would nip at the hind end of the other, and just like that, the newly tagged canine would tear off after the other, barking like mad and giving off every notion that they alone were warding off the devil himself. Every so often, twin streaks of fire would come frighteningly close to our legs as we continued to explore the vineyards.

"They sure are having fun, aren't they?" I mused.

"I'll say. Did you know that Sherlock has a rider?"

"Is that so? Wow. I didn't even see her. She must be crouched low. Here's the million-dollar question: does Sherlock know she's there?"

The hitchhiker in question was a small, African grey parrot by the name of Ruby. She had originally belonged to one Clara Hansen, a woman I was ashamed to admit I had bad-mouthed on more than one occasion. Well, karma had a way of rearing its ugly head. Clara had passed away and guess who ended up taking care of the bird?

Yours truly.

I had originally thought Ruby wouldn't be able to get along with the two corgis, but much to my surprise, the three of them had become the Three Stooges. Ruby, as Jillian had just pointed out, had started a new habit: corgi riding. She was known to settle on Sherlock's back, and nothing short of a bath would remove her if she didn't want to be moved. The dogs came zipping by us for a third time. There, crouched low in the center of Sherlock's back, and bopping her head up and down as parrots were wont to do when they were excited, was Ruby. I'd try to take a picture of the three of them but somehow, they always know when I'm trying to capture a Kodak moment and the opportunity would be over.

"I gotta tell you," I began, as we turned to follow the line of marionberry bushes running east, "I really had a good time in England. Yes, it was a little rushed, and yes, some incredibly remarkable events happened."

Jillian nodded. "I couldn't agree more. Where are you going with this?"

"Well, it's just that …"

"Itching to head out traveling once more?" my new wife guessed.

"Is it a bad thing?" I asked. "Yes, I love our life here, and I love what the two of us have created. It's … that is to say, I guess …"

"… you enjoy traveling," Jillian finished for me. "There's nothing wrong with that."

"What about you?" I countered. "If I were to ask you what country you'd most like to visit, what would your answer be?"

There was no hesitation whatsoever.

"New Zealand."

My ears perked up. Being a huge Middle Earth fan, I've always wanted to go see the filming locations from Lord of the Rings and the Hobbit trilogy. So, the question was, did my significant other know this, or is this just a fluke coincidence?

"The look on your face says you're interested," Jillian observed, giving me a warm smile. "That makes me happy. New Zealand it is. We'll just have to decide on a time of the year to go."

The corgis tore by me again. Yes, Sherlock still had his rider with him. In fact, I could hear Ruby squawking with glee as they disappeared behind a row of blueberry bushes.

"Thankfully," my wife continued, "you and the dogs haven't worked a case in a while. May I presume that levels of crime in Pomme Valley are returning to those not seen since before the BZ era?"

I snorted with exasperation. "BZ? Not you, too, dear."

In case you haven't figured it out yet, BZ stood for *Before Zack*. It's an acronym Vance Samuelson, my good friend who's a detective in the local police force, coined to delineate when the levels of crime skyrocketed. It just so happened to coincide with my arrival in town.

Jillian giggled. "I'm just teasing you, Zachary. I'm only trying to point out that your skills as a police consultant haven't been called into play recently."

"Skills as a consultant?" I repeated, shaking my head. "I think you mean skills as a dog handler."

Right on cue, Sherlock and Watson appeared, but not from around the nearest row of bushes, which is what you'd think. No, Sherlock decided, for whatever reason, to *push* his way through the bush. Uh, oh. Was he trying to dislodge his passenger?

"Careful, pal. Are you trying to shake Ruby? That's not very nice."

We both heard the cackle of laughter coming from Sherlock's direction. Jillian tapped my shoulder and pointed at my tri-colored dog's stomach. There, hanging upside down, with tufts of fur clutched tightly in her claws, was Ruby.

"Come on out of there," I ordered. "I'll call her to my

shoulder. That way, she'll leave you alone for a bit."

Sherlock complied, giving himself a good shaking as he did so. Just as soon as the corgi became still, Ruby was back in position. Whistling once, I tapped my arm. The little parrot immediately abandoned her perch and flew to my shoulder.

"Hey there, Ruby. Let's give Sherlock a break for now, okay?"

"Give us a kiss, Precious! Give us a kiss!"

"That bird sure does adore you," Jillian said, as she reached up to give Ruby a friendly pat.

"It must be my magnetic personality," I quipped. "But, you're right. The dogs and I haven't worked a case in a while. The last one was, what, the one with the stolen bikes? That was nearly three weeks ago, and I don't think can count as a real case."

"Why not?" Jillian asked.

"Well, it was very anti-climactic. Sherlock led us straight to a kid's house, while he was at home. Turns out the kid was storing the stolen bikes in his garage and selling them online to people in nearby communities. I think Vance said most of his sales were in Medford."

"The stolen bicycles were in the garage?" Jillian said, shaking her head. "You'd think the boy's parents would have noticed. Oh, don't tell me. They were the ringleaders, weren't they? That's horrible."

I placed my hand over hers. "Actually, the boy only had a mother, and she worked all the time. She never parked her car in the garage, so only rarely went in there. She didn't have a clue what her son was up to."

"I can only imagine it didn't go over well," Jillian said.

I laughed. "Oh, it didn't. That mother was so angry

that Vance had to warn her not to do anything, unless she wanted to be wearing handcuffs, too. But, it all worked out. The son agreed to track down all the bikes he had sold and give them back to their rightful owners."

Jillian nodded. "Good. So, is that what's the matter with you?"

"Hmm?"

"Zachary, I do believe you're bored."

"What? Me? Bored? Pssht."

"Pssht?"

The sound of my wife mimicking my sound of exasperation had me grinning.

"Maybe I am," I admitted.

"Are the sales of *Heart of Éire* still doing good?"

I nodded. "Still burning up the charts. You'll hear no complaints from either me or Vance, for that matter."

"Are you going to write a sequel?"

Heart of Éire came to life as an anniversary present from Vance to his wife, Tori, only I'm the one who wrote it. Yes, it was Vance's idea, but I'm the one who took that idea and fleshed it out into a full-fledged novel. That was why I was splitting the royalties with him, fifty-fifty.

"No, I don't think so. The story was wrapped up fairly tightly, all issues were addressed, and the characters had closure with each other and their situations. It doesn't need a sequel."

"So, what book are you going to work on next?"

"Ah, I see what you're doing. You're trying to get me involved on a project, so I'll stop moping around. Is that it?"

Jillian laughed again. "Guilty as charged. I know you're never so happy as when you're fully immersed in a new story, so I'm hoping to hear that the next book you'll be working on will be something new for you."

I nodded. "As a matter of fact, I think I will be setting my next novel in Scotland. Maybe the Scottish Highlands?"

Much to my surprise, my wife was shaking her head no.

"That's been done to death, Zachary."

"All right, that's a fair point."

"What about Loch Ness?"

My ears perked up. "Loch Ness? What about it?"

"Could you set your next book at Loch Ness? Could you come up with some type of fitting story? After all, if memory serves, it's located in the Highlands."

Loch Ness, in Scotland, as a setting for a book? Now *that* I could get on board with. A smile spread across my face.

"I'll have to do some serious thinking about that one. I'll admit, I do like the idea. Should I make it another romance, or try my hand at something new again?"

It was Jillian's turn to perk up. "Something new? Like what?"

"I don't know. What about … well, how about a murder mystery? Loch Ness would make a great setting for someone to get offed by some unusual method."

"Does it have to be murder?" Jillian asked, frowning. "What about a heist? Or … I know! How about some type of paranormal romance?"

"Paranormal? As in, have a mortal fall in love with someone who isn't?"

"What do you think?" Jillian asked.

"Let me think about it. Loch Ness and the Inverness area are absolutely gorgeous. If I set a book in that area, I want to make darn certain I do the area, and its history, justice."

Jillian slipped her arm through mine. "Good answer, Mr. Anderson."

"Why, thank you, Mrs. Anderson."

My phone chose that time to ring.

"Hello? Oh, hey Caden. What's up, pal? You what? You're where? Oh, all right. Jillian and I are in Berry Central. We'll be home in about ten minutes."

"Is everything okay?" Jillian wanted to know, as I terminated the call.

"Yeah, he wants to talk shop. Apparently, there are a few things he wants to run by me."

"I see. Well, I can …"

"Oh, no you don't," I protested, as Jillian started to pull away from me. "You're part owner of the winery now. Let's hear what he has to say."

What my winemaster had to say, however, wasn't good. Oh, don't get me wrong, provided I go along, it'll be very good for Lentari Cellars. However, as was always the case whenever Caden wanted to talk to me, it meant he was going after my checkbook. I was going to be asked to spend more money, and I had only one question about it: was there a comma in the price tag?

The answer was yes, by the way.

"We need to expand, Zachary," Caden began, the moment Jillian and I sank down on the couch in the living room. Sherlock and Watson promptly went for their toys and began a tug-of-war match with a plush animal that was never designed to be pulled from opposite directions. "Guys? It's a toy, not food. Don't destroy it, all right? I'm sorry, Caden. You were saying something about wanting to expand? Isn't that what we did when I bought those extra thirty-five acres? You can't possibly tell me we need more land. In fact, I think we still have some fields without anything in them!"

Jillian placed a reassuring hand over my own. "Calm down, Zachary. I have a feeling Caden's request isn't about land, but manpower."

Caden grinned at Jillian. "Yes, exactly! I have LC running practically from morning to night, squeezing every last drop we can get out of our grapes, and yet, we still can't keep up with demand."

"Out with it, pal," I sighed. "How many and what's it gonna cost me?"

"Us," Jillian corrected, "and if you'll let Caden finish, perhaps he could tell us?"

"Oh, I'm going to like having you in the picture," Caden said, as he nodded his appreciation at my wife. "Okay, Jillian is right. We need more staff. If I have a couple of extra bodies, then we can start using those extra vats you purchased last year."

"We're not using them now?" I asked, bewildered.

"Nope. How could we? By the time I could get around to bringing in those extra holding tanks, then the existing holding tanks would have already been processed, and they become superfluous."

"Nice word," I muttered, eliciting a grin from my winery's caretaker. "I get it. You need more hands. Well, the winery has been turning a decent profit for quite some time now. I have no problems upgrading the word to *hefty*. What do you propose?"

"I'd like to hire at least two more people," Caden nervously began.

"Full-time or part-time?" Jillian wanted to know.

"I was going to start with part, and hopefully move them to full should they prove to be good workers."

"What about our two interns?" I asked, as I thought of our high school students who had been with the winery for a while now. "How are they doing?"

Jillian giggled. "Honey, I do believe he's referring to hiring the interns full-time. Isn't that right, Mr. Burne?"

"That's exactly right, and please call me Caden. 'Mr. Burne' creeps me out. Zack, you like Doug and Kim, don't you?"

"Shouldn't we let them graduate from high school first before we corral them into a life of servitude here?" I asked.

Caden sighed and shook his head. "Zack, they *did* graduate. Last summer. I actually approached them and inquired whether or not they'd like to continue building experience here. Both of them responded with a resounding yes."

"They already graduated," I groaned. "Man, that makes me feel old."

"You *are* old," Jillian teased.

"Pssht. As for those two," I said, nodding, "they're both good workers. I have no problems with this. Go ahead, I'll leave the details to you. Just let me know how much and where to send the paychecks. As soon as you give me the info, I'll pass it along to my accountant."

"You got it. You rock, Zack. Jillian? Welcome to Lentari Cellars!"

"Why thank you, Mr. ... I mean, Caden."

The two of us watched Caden hurry for the door, presumably to make two former interns very happy. Right at that time, both corgis dropped the toys they had been playing with and looked directly at me, as though I had just grown a tail.

"What?" I demanded. "If you two are smelling something, then I can tell you it isn't me. Or her. It's probably you guys, you little boogers."

Sherlock continued to stare at me. Or, more specifically, at my shoulder. Ruby was still there. The little parrot had her head tucked under a wing and was seemingly sleeping.

"What?" I repeated, although I did lower my voice. "Is there something wrong?"

"My b-bounty is as b-boundless as the sea."

"Did you say something?" Jillian asked, as she turned to look at me.

"I didn't say anything, but I did hear something."

Jillian and I shared a look before turning to regard the bird sitting on my shoulder. Ruby had just awoken and given herself a good shake. She must have learned that particular behavior from Sherlock and Watson.

"Did Ruby just say something?" Jillian asked.

Then, with a shrill screech, Ruby repeated the strange phrase in a much louder voice.

"My b-bounty is as b-boundless as the sea."

TWO

The next day began with me taking a hard look at the comfortable, spacious living room in my house, located in Lentari Cellars. There was the couch where I've spent countless hours cuddling the dogs. It was also where Jillian and I have spent a lot of time together, sharing the events in our day, watching a movie, and so on. Opposite the couch was the matching blue floral loveseat, which was where we typically sat whenever our friends were over. Completing the seating possibilities were two worn, plush armchairs, also decorated in a (faded) floral pattern.

Clearly, Aunt Bonnie—the woman I inherited the house and winery from—enjoyed her floral prints.

Was this something I really wanted to get rid of? Did I have any business giving away—or donating—all the furniture in this house? I mean, yes, it was mine, free and clear, but what if there were sentimental attachments to some of these pieces? Should I reach out and see if anyone from that side of the family would like to take it off my hands?

Then, my gaze returned to the couch and dropped to the ground. That was where Sherlock had hidden my phone, after being held at gun-point by a crazy reporter. And over there? I could see the stone fireplace, where Jillian and I shared our first Christmas together. It was also one of the places where I confessed to Jillian that I wasn't going to let anything happen to her when I believed someone could have been after her.

There, okay? See what's happening here? For every good memory I have, there are also negative experiences tagging right along. I think it would do me good to be able to raze this place to the ground so that we …

You *did* know that's what I was talking about earlier, didn't you? When I said what the two of us were proposing would cost thousands of dollars, I meant it. After all, we're talking about tearing down Aunt Bonnie's farm house and building a brand new, Jillian-approved, manor in its place. And, based on everything the two of us wanted in a house, our new home is going to be super-expensive. The Victorian manor Jillian thought we were going to build was a little over three thousand square feet of living space. Well, after careful consideration, I decided to upgrade the plans to the very first set I caught her looking at, which was a mansion so large that we would essentially be living in our own zip code. Seriously, the plans actually stated that the architect drew them up for French nobility. And the size? Get a load of this: over seven thousand square feet. It's more than enough for all the goodies I had an architect secretly add.

As for the current house, well, I had no problem signing the paperwork to tear it down. Was I worried about what *that* side of the family was going to say? No. They could kiss my ... well, let's just say that I wasn't going to lose any sleep over it. The only *slight* dilemma I had found myself faced with was, should I, or shouldn't I, reach out to the Davies family and offer them their pick of furniture? After all, there might be some type of sentimental attachment to some of the pieces.

Right about then, I remembered what Burt Johnson had told me. The owner of Hidden Relic Antiques had somehow learned of what we were planning on doing and reached out to see if he could tour the house and collect the things he thought he could sell. Jillian and I agreed almost immediately. So, if Bonnie's family wanted any of the furnishings in here, then they could buy them off of Burt and my conscience would remain clear. After all, hadn't that particular family gone on record—many times—as saying they wished I was either dead or out of the picture? Wasn't it the late Abigail Lawson, Bonnie's daughter, who had tried numerous times to wrest control of the estate away from me? So ... no, I had no moral obligation to do jack squat for that family.

Satisfied with my decision, I pulled out my phone, intent on sending a message to my wife. I knew Jillian was here, at the winery somewhere, but I didn't know where. Not really wanting to go traipsing around until I found her, I was halfway through typing a message to her when she appeared in the doorway. One of her girlfriends, Hannah, owner of PV's one and only florist shop, was hot on her heels.

"It's way too soon!" Hannah was saying. "I'm not ready

for this!"

"Trust me, you are," Jillian set her purse on the kitchen counter and turned to face her friend. "Your divorce is final. You said it yourself. It's not good to keep holed up inside Apple Blossoms for hours on end. You've got to get out there and *live*."

"But … oh! Zack! I didn't see you there."

"Don't mind me. I just came in here to grab a s--" My eyes widened as I realized I almost revealed what I was looking to acquire. Plastering the biggest, sheepish grin on my face that I could, and jamming both my hands in my pockets, I tried to backtrack as best as I could. Unfortunately, my mind drew a blank once both sets of female eyes landed on me. "Ummm …"

"Zachary Michael, you've had your one soda for the day. I told you I wouldn't be the Fun Police, and I know cutting down your soda intake is hard for you, but this is only the second day. I thought you'd at least *try* to make it through the end of the week having no more than one soda a day."

"But, I didn't have one today!" I protested. "I can't get into trouble if I haven't …"

"And the can of Pepsi you took with you when you took the dogs for a walk?" Jillian smoothly interrupted me.

Oh, snap. Truth be told, I *had* forgotten about that one. Man, now I'm going to come across as a scheming caffeine junkie coming up with any excuse to get his next fix.

"He's telling the truth," Hannah promptly reported. "Look at his face. He forgot about that one."

"Is that true?" Jillian asked, as she stepped in front of me. "Did you actually forget you drank a can of soda today?"

"Ummm …?"

Jillian sighed, chuckled once, and turned to her friend. "I think I'll start slipping some gingko tablets into his soda. Maybe that would help his memory?"

I made a motion as though I was checking something off an invisible list. "Watch what I drink from now on. Got it."

Jillian gazed at my face a few moments before she sobered. "Are you all right?"

"I am," I confirmed, and then held up my phone. "I didn't know where you were, and was about ready to send you a message."

"Oh? What about?"

"I can leave, if you'd like," Hannah quickly said.

I grinned at Jillian's friend and shook my head. "It's okay. You can stay. My dear? You mentioned that you didn't want to do anything about this house until you were certain I was all okay with it, right?"

Jillian nodded. "That's right. Wait. Are you saying you are, or are you saying you aren't?"

I held out my phone. "I'm ready to make the call. They were simply waiting on me, so once I give them permission, demo can begin within a week or two."

My wife's eyes lit up. "Seriously? You're not going to feel guilty about it, are you?"

"Not in the slightest," I confirmed. "I don't owe that family anything. If there's anything they want in here, well, they can purchase it back from our friend Burt. So, if you'd do the honors, let's get Burt and his team out here to see if there's anything he wants."

"How much are we going to charge him?" Jillian asked, as she pulled out her phone.

"Not one cent. If he wants it, then it's his."

"That's very generous of you," Hannah observed. "Are you two doing some remodeling in here?"

I made the slicing motion across my throat. "Everything gets the pink slip. Jillian and I have decided to tear this house down and build something tailored to our preferences."

Hannah whistled. "Wow. That's going to be expensive."

"It is," I said, nodding, "but worth it. This way, it'll be something the two of us can plan out, detail by detail."

"So, you're getting rid of everything in here?"

"I am. I barely brought any of my own things to this house, seeing how it was already furnished when I got it. So, whatever Burt doesn't want, or take, is going to be donated to … Hannah? You keep staring at me. Is there something in here you'd like for your place?"

It was Hannah's turn to appear sheepish. "I really shouldn't. I have no business asking, so I should just …"

"Hannah?" Jillian interrupted. "If there's something in here that you'd like, then please, just ask."

"Seconded," I added.

"Well, it's just that Colin's bed is getting old, and I was thinking about getting him a new one."

Jillian was already nodding. "The bed in the guest room upstairs would be perfect for him. He's a growing boy. He's old enough to have a queen-sized bed."

"And you really don't mind me taking it off your hands?" Hannah asked, as she continued to bite her lip with apprehension.

"If anything, I'd be glad to pay *you* to take it off my hands," I joked. Right about then, I heard a chime. Was it coming from me, or was one of the girls responsible for it? "I don't think that was me."

Both Jillian and Hannah checked their phones.

"Not us," Hannah reported.

I pulled out my own phone. There, on the display, was the notification: it was time to leave in order to make the appointment with Harry.

"Ruby? Where are you? It's time for your checkup." I heard a soft trill, and then my phone went off again, only when I pulled it back out to look, there was nothing there. "Stinker. Was that you, Ruby?" My phone chimed again. And again. "Okay, ha, you got me. Now, come on. We need to go talk to Harry. Are you going to come peacefully?"

The little gray parrot squawked once, and I finally spotted her, on top of the nearest bookcase. She bobbed her head as she watched me pull out a small pet carrier from a nearby closet. When it came to going in for checkups, meaning the little parrot was required to ride inside a carrier, I had a fifty-fifty shot of a drama free excursion. Sometimes the bird would cry bloody murder. Other times, Ruby would squawk with pleasure at the thought of going for a ride. This time, thankfully, she hopped right into the carrier and gave me a wolf whistle.

"Really? Was that necessary?"

Ruby made a screeching noise, which sounded an awful lot like a maniacal cackle, and we were ready. Kissing Jillian as I walked out the door, I caught sight of the corgis and pointed at the leashes.

"Wanna go for a …?"

Sherlock and Watson quickly lined up, as though I was a drill sergeant preparing to conduct an inspection. Once the dogs were secure in my Jeep, we were off. Since the weather was nice, I had the windows partly down—and locked—as we pulled into town. Parking at Harry's clinic, I looked back at the dogs and gave them each a pat.

"This shouldn't take long. I just need to make sure she's okay. The last thing I need to worry about is a bird spewing out gibberish. Ruby? Are you ready?"

"Give us a kiss, Precious! Give us a kiss!"

"I'll take that as a yes."

All the way into town, Ruby said her same catch phrase over and over. Was I jumping the gun? Did I really want Harry smirking at me for bringing in a bird who clearly repeated something she had heard? I just don't have a clue how she could've picked that particular phrase up. Maybe from something we were watching on television? Although, according to Jillian, it was something neither of us have heard recently.

Hence, the trip to the vet.

"Zack! Hey bro, how's it goin'?"

Harrison Watt, veterinarian for Pomme Valley, was my best friend from high school. Knowing him back then, and seeing him now, continues to blow my mind. Harry liked to party, which inevitably led to getting into trouble, and coming *thiiiiiis* close to flunking out of school. Yet, all it took for him to turn his life around was his future wife, Julie, standing by him after he got himself into a terrible car wreck. Now, he gets to wear the white jacket.

"Did I read those notes right? What's goin' on with Ruby? Did she get into something she shouldn't have?"

"Well, she started …"

"Let's go to room three."

Following Harry into one of the exam rooms, I gently placed the pet carrier on the examination table and opened the door. Ruby appeared almost immediately. She bobbed her head a few times before flying to my shoulder.

"She sure is an affectionate little thing," Harry observed. "So, what's she doin'?"

"Look, she's a parrot, and I know she's got a habit of repeating what she hears," I began, "but just yesterday she said something that I've never heard before."

"Probably picked up something someone said," Harry began, as he gently took the bird from my shoulder. "Let's check your wings, darlin'."

Used to Harry's checkups, Ruby didn't resist.

"I thought of that, too," I admitted, "only what she said was really strange. It's not something Jillian or myself would have ever said."

"What'd she say?" Harry asked, as he gently extended each wing and felt its skeletal structure. Grunting, he switched wings.

"Something about boundless seas," I said, as I scratched my chin.

"Boundless seas? Are you sure you weren't watching some type of travel program and Ruby overheard? Maybe it was a commercial."

"If it was, then it's not any commercial I can recall."

"Boundless seas," Harry repeated. "I don't know, bro. It sounds familiar to me. How much of it can you remember?"

"I believe it was something along the lines of bounties being as boundless as the sea."

"Now I *know* I've heard that somewhere," Harry began. "That's just great. It's probably gonna bug me until I remember where it's from."

"You're that sure you've heard the phrase before?"

Harry nodded. After a few moments, he pulled his phone from his pocket and tapped the screen a few times.

"There you go. I told you I knew it. My bounty is as boundless as the sea? It's Shakespearean. Juliet said it to Romeo. Had to read it in school, bro. It was terrible."

I looked back at Ruby just in time to see Harry slip his phone into his pocket and resume his examination of her.

"It's a line from Romeo and Juliet?" I said, as I crossed my arms over my chest. "You're kidding. Well, I can now say with one hundred percent certainty that Ruby did *not* hear that particular phrase at my house. I never read that much Shakespeare, and know next to nothing about him. Jillian, perhaps, but not me."

"Maybe Jillian was streaming something about Shakespeare?" Harry suggested. "A documentary, maybe?" He finished his examination of Ruby's wings and moved on to her beak. Rubbing a finger gently across the parrot's face, he reached behind him to pull out a drawer in the examination table and retrieve what looked like a Dremel kit. "Don't you worry, little lady. We'll get you looking all pretty again."

"What are you doing?" I asked.

"Her beak is looking a bit long. Thought I'd trim it up for you."

"Her beak is long? Since when?"

"Dude, a bird's beak never stops growin', bro. Just like your fingernails, they gotta be trimmed."

"Huh. You learn something new every day. Well, how does hers look?"

"Just fine. I figure you're giving her those pieces of wood like I suggested the first time you brought her in."

"Harry, she shreds them, like a cat with a scratching post. Is a bird supposed to do that?"

"Relax, bro. Birds gnaw on things in order to groom

their beaks. It's nothing to worry about."

Firing up the device which looked and sounded like a dentist's drill, Harry carefully trimmed Ruby's beak, taking what I would estimate as a quarter-inch off the upper beak. Ruby, thankfully, must have been familiar with this process, because she didn't move a muscle or make the slightest of fits. Once he was done, Ruby hopped over to my hand, as though she needed some emotional support after experiencing such a harrowing ordeal.

"You're fine, Ruby. You did good. I'm proud of you. Except for the Shakespeare quotes. I don't suppose you'd care to tell me where you picked that line up from, would you?"

"Give us a kiss, Precious! Give us a kiss!"

"Do you two need a moment alone, bro?" Harry chuckled.

"Hysterical, pal. Hey, I know Ruby is fond of me, and I'll do what I can for her, but what prevents her from simply flying away? I've always wondered that."

Harry reached out and gently extended one of Ruby's wings. The little gray parrot eyed my friend, as though she was wondering why he was looking at her wings again, but didn't object.

"Do you see these feathers here? And these long ones down here?"

"Well, they aren't that long, are they?" I pointed out.

"Exactly, bro. Keep these feathers trimmed and you take away the possibility of flight. Her feathers, just like her beak, are always growing. You don't like long nails, do you? Well, neither does she."

I silently watched as Harry, inspecting her wings for a third time, reached into the same drawer that had the

Dremel, and pulled out a pair of metal scissors. A few snips here and there, and it was over.

"I'm still not convinced what you just did wasn't cruel."

"Do you think Ruby would be able to care for herself out there, on her own?" Harry asked. I also got the distinct impression he was using his lecture voice, the same he reserved for elementary school appearances during the year. "She's domesticated, bro. She wouldn't survive. So, we make sure she's not tempted."

"And the feathers will grow back?"

"Yup. That's why I typically trim them whenever you bring her in. It doesn't hurt her, and is actually good for her."

"So, as far as you can tell, there's nothing wrong with Ruby?"

Harry ruffled the feathers on the top of Ruby's head, eliciting a squawk from the little parrot, and leaned back, against the examination table.

"She's in perfect health, bro. There's nothing for me to diagnose, so there's nothing for you to worry about."

"And if she starts spouting lines from famous tragedies again?"

"Record it and put it online? I don't know, Zack. I think it's just a little harmless fun for her."

Thanking my friend and paying the bill for services rendered, we headed home. The moment we were inside my Jeep, Ruby pecked at the pet carrier's gate a few times. Figuring she had been traumatized enough, and verifying all windows were closed, I let the poor girl out. Ruby immediately fluttered over to Sherlock, who was curled up behind me, and settled onto his back. Moments later, the little parrot had snuggled down, into Sherlock's soft fur, and tucked her beak under her wing. Glancing over at Watson, I noticed that she, too, was sleeping. In fact, neither of the two dogs had bothered to wake up once I was back in the car.

Looking at the three animals sleeping in the backseat of my Jeep, I shook my head. Oh, what I would give to lead a dog's life. Well, one of my dogs, that is.

Pulling away from Third Street, we turned left on Main, but not before I heard a woof. Unsurprisingly, it had come from Sherlock, who was now standing on his hind legs, much to the annoyance of his avian passenger, and staring out the window.

"Woof!"

"What is it, boy? Do you see something?"

Sherlock woofed again. It wasn't loud enough to wake Watson, but it was still curious enough to have me reaching for my phone. After I snapped a few pictures, Sherlock settled down and went back to sleep. What was Sherlock playing at? We weren't working on any case, yet he sure acted like it. He had settled down the moment I had taken pictures of whatever was in the direction Sherlock was looking. That was something he didn't do unless we were actively working on *something*. I'll have to ask Jillian about it later.

Once I made it home, I noticed right away that Jillian's car was gone. It wasn't surprising. Jillian worked very hard to keep her store, Cookbook Nook, in tip-top shape. That meant she put in some long hours, thus allowing me some free time to myself. In this case, it was time to go over the final set of plans.

What plans, you ask? Well, as I mentioned earlier, I was planning on tearing down this country farmhouse I had inherited, all the way to the foundation, and even that was going to get broken up and removed. What were we putting in place? Yes, I mentioned a manor, but I don't think you have any idea *what* type of manor it's going to have.

Let me show you.

Returning to the house, I walked to my office on the second floor and carefully opened up the closet. Stashed between my black dinner jacket and the matching black business shirt—which comprised my one and only formal attire, were the meticulously drawn blueprints for our new house.

Our house. It felt good to say it. Jillian and I finally came to an agreement on what to do with our houses. Mine would be torn down, while hers would be either transformed into a bed and breakfast, like Highland House, or else the house would be kept as is, in preparation for a few of our family members who were getting up there in years. But, as for the new plans, well, Jillian didn't know about even *half* of the cool features that were going to be installed. Secret passages from one end of the house to the other, like the Clue mansion, from the movie. I was putting in a secret reading room/library for Jillian. It would be a nice, comfortable place for the two of us to go to lose ourselves in a good book. And, of course, I couldn't forget my Bat Cave. The new house was going to have a large basement. There'd be multiple access points to enter the basement, which was going to be outfitted with a sound-proof theater, a retro arcade, and if I could find a couple of machines for sale, several Skee ball games.

Yeah, I know what some of you must be thinking right about now. Isn't that a waste of money? Well, for me, it's a chance to relive my childhood. I spent many happy memories in those old mall arcades, and I would consider it a dream come true to be able to have something similar in my own house.

I've also been pushing like crazy to get one of those Flav-O-Matic soda dispensers installed, but I can't help but feel like it'd be more of a hassle than it's worth. Jillian suggested installing an honest-to-goodness coin-operated soda machine, and thus far, I'm leaning toward that option. It'd be charging no more than a quarter per can, of course. After all, I wasn't going to bleed myself dry, was I?

Then again, this monstrosity was going to have over seventy-five hundred square feet of living space, six bedrooms, four boat-deep garage bays large enough to hold a total of eight mid-size cars, and enough bathrooms to put a hotel to shame. Before you ask if I've lost what little common sense I have left, why would the two of us want a house so big? Well, Jillian picked this set of plans from the start, but then backed out when she thought she heard me groan at the proposed price tag. However, in my defense, it wasn't a groan, but a grunt. Our parents are getting up there in age. It was time to start thinking long term, meaning more than likely, we were going to have parents living with us. Now, I don't have a problem with family members living in the same house, but I would prefer said house to have plenty of room, so we're each not intruding on the other's space. Therefore, each of the bedrooms was going to be the size of a suite, and each suite was going to have its own bathroom.

See? There's a method to my madness.

But, I also want to make it fun. If you're not familiar with all the secrets of Highland House, I urge you to look it up and see for yourself where my inspiration is coming from. I think every man alive would love to have a house with a secret or two hidden about. Well, in my case, they were going to number more than that. Jillian just doesn't know it yet.

Therefore, I sat down at my desk and started making calls. I arranged for the movers, first, to take what little things of my own I actually had in the house and move them to a storage unit. Next up, I called Burt Johnson, from Hidden Relics Antiques, and told him to meet me at the house tomorrow and to bring a truck. He gladly obliged, by the way. Then, I arranged for a local hospice to come by and pick up whatever was left: furniture, clothing, pots and pans, and so on. Then, a call to the contractor confirmed a week from next Monday was still open for them to begin demolition. That'd give me enough time to get everything out of the house that I wanted to save.

My phone rang just then. A smile appeared as I saw the name.

"Well, if it isn't the prettiest lady in the whole wide world. What can I do for you, my dear?"

"I can certainly get used to you answering the phone like that," Jillian giggled. "I was just calling to see if you'd like to get some lunch with me. I have some free time coming up in about an hour, and thought we haven't been to the Lonely Gringo in a while. It's under new management, so I'd like to give them another try."

The last time we tried the food, it was bland, the chips were stale and overcooked, and the staff was … indifferent. We both figured it might've just been bad luck, but a follow up visit nearly a month later had us both swearing off our once favorite Mexican food joint until something changed. So, the suggestion we should give them another try filled me with hope.

"I'm game if you are. I certainly hope their menu has gone back to what it was. Better yet, I hope that whichever chef they were using the last time we were there was fired."

"Oh, you won't need to worry about him."

Curiosity piqued, I started to laugh. "You had a hand in this, didn't you?"

"Whatever could you mean, Zachary?"

"Mm-hmm. Listen, there's something I need to tell you."

"Oh? I'm listening."

"Two weeks from now, Aunt Bonnie's house will be gone."

"Oooo! How exciting! I'm so very glad to hear you're moving quickly on this. I'm anxious to get our new Victorian manor built."

"Yeah, about that."

"Is something the matter?"

"Well, do you remember that day when we were looking at plans?"

"Yes."

"Including the first set? Well, that's the one that's going to be built."

"The first set? As in, the French mansion? Oooo, how exciting! That must mean … you're going to put in your Bat Cave, aren't you?"

I rustled the blueprints I was staring at. "They're already included on the plans."

"I love you, you silly man. Go ahead. I'll swing by after work and help you pack up some things. You're going to love living in Carnation Cottage! Well, for a few months, anyway."

"You're the best, my dear. I'll plan on meeting you at

the Lonely Gringo. Let's say around …"

"*Virginity b-breeds mites, much like a ch-cheese.*"

"What did you say, Zachary?"

"That wasn't me, I swear it."

"You have the television on?" Jillian guessed.

"No, I don't. I think … I think that was Ruby again."

"*Virginity b-breeds mites, much like a ch-cheese.*"

"Yeah, I heard it the first time. Ruby? Where are you? Why did you say that?"

I heard a soft fluttering of wings. The little grey parrot appeared, flapping like mad in order to gain some altitude so she could land on my shoulder. She nuzzled the side of my face and fell silent.

"Has she said anything else?" Jillian wanted to know.

"Nope, just that weird sentence about virgins."

"What did she say again? Something about virginity? Zachary Michael, what are you subjecting that poor bird to?"

I held up my hands in protest, even though my lovely wife couldn't see me. And, of course, I felt my face flame up.

"Hey, I'm innocent! I don't know where she's getting this."

Both corgis came trotting in the room, sat next to my desk, and then stared at Ruby, as though I had called them over and wanted their opinion.

"I heard doggie toenails. Sherlock and Watson are there now, aren't they?"

"They are," I confirmed, "and they're acting an awful lot like they're working a case. They're staring straight at Ruby, as though it's the first time they've ever seen her. It's the strangest thing."

"Zachary? I think it might be time we look into the meaning of these quotes."

THREE

W here would you like it? Hey, excuse me? Where can I put this ... and no one is listening to me. Swell. Hey, could someone please indicate where ... and would you look at that? I'm still talking to myself."

Somewhat annoyed no one was paying attention to the pack mule hauling stuff in from storage, I placed both folding tables I was holding onto the floor, right smack in the middle of the room, and waited for someone to say something. After all, Jillian was the one who had asked me to help her set up for a last-minute event she was going to hold in her store. Cookbook Nook has, on various occasions, held cookbook author signing events or demonstrations, and this would usually mean a number of tables would have to be brought in. The visiting author would then set up their equipment and make a few recipes from their cookbook. Now that I think about it, that's how Jillian and I first met, during a demonstration for a local author who had struck it big.

Brings back memories. But, I digress. Back to the story at hand.

As luck would have it, this touring cookbook author was some type of food celeb, and was supposed to be holding her event at a bookstore in Medford, only the store was having some technical difficulties and couldn't make itself available in time. And, since Jillian clearly knows everyone in the state, the owner of that store practically begged my wife to host it at Cookbook Nook. Never one to turn down the chance to make a tidy profit, Jillian readily accepted. And that meant yours truly had just been drafted into service.

Oh, well, I really didn't mind. I enjoyed spending time at the store because, well, that meant I got to spend time with Jillian. However, I haven't seen much of her in the last couple of hours because of the myriad details demanding her attention in preparation for this visit. Whoever was visiting must really have a large following, because so far, I have helped empty—and move—no fewer than six different display racks. Most of the aisles of books, I was shocked to discover, had a very unique construction to them. I didn't even know the racks were repositionable until I helped one of the girls move them.

Each rack of books was nearly ten feet long, and I'd say about five feet high. The endcaps of these displays had wheels on them, and if you inserted these special tools, which looked like hydraulic floor jacks one might find in an automobile body shop, and pushed the bar into the locked *down* position, then the entire endcap was lifted up and temporarily locked in place. Do the same thing to the other end, and just like that, the display became movable. Get someone on either end of the display and suddenly, the racks could be moved, all without emptying the shelves.

After moving the necessary number of racks out of the way, it was just a matter of bringing in all the folding tables from Jillian's storeroom, located at the back of the store. And that is precisely what I had been doing, only without someone to tell me where the tables should be set up—and *how*—I was now just some lumbering idiot in the way.

My thoughts drifted back to Ruby. Yesterday's blurb about virgins was the second phrase she had said that I hadn't ever heard before. Virginity and cheese? I mean, are you serious? Where the heck had that little parrot picked up that particular line? It sure wasn't at my house.

I felt a tap on my shoulder. Turning, I saw one of Jillian's employees. Sydney, I believe. The freckled, redheaded teenager was smiling at me and waiting expectantly. The question is, waiting for what?

"Wow, you sure are lost in your thoughts, aren't you, Mr. Anderson?" the teenager gushed.

I shrugged. "Guilty as charged."

"Are you all right?" Sydney asked. "You and Mrs. Anderson are, uh, doing okay, aren't you?"

I smiled at the girl. "Of course. Sorry, you're right. I am a bit distracted. You know who Ruby is, don't you? The African grey parrot I inherited after her previous owner, er, died?"

Sydney bobbed her head. "Of course. I loved going to A Lazy Afternoon just to play with that parrot. It was my favorite bookstore. Still is, I guess. You're her owner now? I should've known. Some people get all the luck."

"Uh-huh. Listen, you sound like you're a good person to ask about this. Did Ruby ever say anything that sounded like gibberish to you? I guess what I'm asking is, did she ever come up with phrases on her own?"

Much to my dismay, Sydney was shaking her head even before I could finish asking the question.

"Oh, no, Ruby only repeats what she hears."

"Yeah, I was afraid of that," I groaned.

Sydney indicated I should pick up the tables and follow her deeper into the store. "I take it she's said something strange?"

Realizing I hadn't heard from either dog in a while, I turned to look back at the recently cleared sitting area. The recliners had been pushed back against the far wall and there, claiming one plush chair apiece, were Sherlock and Watson, watching me intently. Of course, I should mention that they had a long string of admirers. The good thing about that is neither dog was allowed to fall asleep. Every time they drifted off, another fan would appear and give them a thorough scratching.

"I still maintain it's nonsense; gibberish. Don't worry about it. I think Ruby does that to get more attention from me."

"You have a way with animals, Mr. Anderson," Sydney was saying, as she helped me set up my two folding tables next to the growing line of tables stretching from one side of the store to the other. "You should be a veterinarian!"

I laughed out loud. "Harry has got that covered, thank you very much. I've already got enough on my plate without adding anything else. Hey, are you my assigned helper?"

The teenage girl nodded. "For the foreseeable future, yes."

"That's music to my ears. Come on, there's, like, twenty more tables down there and I have no idea how many we're going to need. Maybe another three or four?"

"Mrs. Anderson says we need them all."

I groaned. "Of course she does. All right, she's the boss. We'd better get going."

Nearly thirty minutes later, the tables were set up, the cooking stations were ready, and I was about to head to the front of the store to find Sherlock and Watson. That's when Sydney surprised me by grabbing my arm and pulling me to a stop.

"I've been dying to ask you something, Mr. Anderson."

"Oh? Fire away, Sydney."

"What was it like?"

"What was *what* like?"

"Getting married in Westminster Abbey! For heaven's sake, you and Mrs. Anderson were married in England! And the Queen! The actual Queen of England was at your wedding!"

"Are you looking for confirmation that it really happened? Well, rest assured, it did. Her Royal Highness is a very nice lady. Sharp as a tack and has a sense of humor to match. I'm still in shock that she was able to get the ceremony live-streamed to the school auditorium. It looked like everyone from town was there."

"I was," Sydney admitted, as a blush crept up her cheeks. "I've always said you two are perfect for each other, Mr. Anderson. You've made her very happy. Don't ever stop, 'kay?"

I grinned at the kid. "You're on. Now, do you have any

idea where the two troublemakers are?"

Sydney turned to point at a surprisingly long line. "Follow the people. You'll find them."

"Excuse me? Is that what this line is for? To meet Sherlock and Watson?"

"Mm-hmm. They're famous now. Everyone wants to meet them. Do you want to hear a theory?"

I turned to the freckled teen and gave her an English-approved, Queen-appropriate neck bow. "I'm all ears."

"I've noticed people come here and don't buy anything. Do you know how rare that used to be?"

"Where are you going with this, Sydney?"

"The corgis! The people are coming to see if Sherlock and Watson are in the store that day. I've even had people ask me if their schedules were posted anywhere, seeing how they had chosen to come in on a day where you and the dogs weren't here."

"Oh, brother. Tell me you made that up."

Sydney drew an X on her chest. "I swear I didn't!"

"Well, if they can draw more people in here, then Jillian will be that much happier about it."

"Don't I know it. I mentioned it to Mrs. Anderson last week and she told me she was aware of it, and like you had guessed, she was quite happy with it. She loves those dogs, too, you know."

"Oh, I do. Thanks for your help, Sydney. It's time to get their Royal Canineships and head outta here."

"Have a good day, Mr. Anderson!" Sydney called, as she headed for the front counter.

Following the line of people that I still maintain were waiting for an open cashier, I found both dogs exactly where I left them: in two of the plush armchairs usually found in the reading area. Sherlock was on his back, with all four paws pointed skyward. A middle-aged couple was standing on either side of him, offering the tri-colored corgi praise and adoration. As for Watson? She was sitting on the lap of a girl the same age as Sydney and was close to falling asleep.

"Really, guys?" I asked, as I put in my appearance.

Sherlock cracked an eye and looked at me. Slowly— ever so slowly—he rolled to his feet and stood up. Giving his two admirers a friendly lick, he jumped down from the chair and started to give himself a thorough shaking when he actually stopped himself halfway through. Knowing my dogs' routines like the back of my hand, to hear one of my corgis break their routine was akin to someone shouting my name as loud as they could.

I stared at Sherlock, but he wasn't looking at me. He wasn't even looking at Watson. Instead, his head was turned and he was staring at something in the direction where I had set up those tables. Perhaps they were setting up food displays?

Watson suddenly jumped down from her position on the teenager's lap and also turned to look further into the store, in the same direction as Sherlock. Neither, from what I could tell, was sniffing the air, but instead, they were gazing at *something*. Again, if I didn't know any better, then I'd say they were working a case and they were staring at something I should be taking a picture of.

"Come on guys, there's nothing that way for you two. It's just a bunch of tables. It's time we were going."

Neither dog budged.

"Sherlock? Watson? What's with you two? Come on. No, don't get all stubborn on me. We need to get going." I tried to look as stern as possible and wait it out to see what the corgis would do. "Come on, guys. Don't make me use my daddy voice. Not out in the public like this."

Apparently, I'm not very intimidating. Sighing, I pulled out my cell and tried to triangulate on what the two of them were looking at. Taking several pictures, I watched both of my dogs lose interest and look up at me, as if I was the hold-up on why we hadn't left yet.

Jillian arrived at my side at that moment. Somehow, and I'm not sure how, she could sense that I was preparing to leave.

"Heading home? That's a good idea. Hey, before you go, could you do me a teensy favor?"

I ended up laughing out loud. "Hit me with your best shot, woman."

To say that my darling wife was more than up to the challenge would be an understatement.

"I'm so glad you asked, Zachary. There's one last thing I was hoping you'd be able to do for me."

"Name it. What's up?"

My wife pointed toward the stairs leading to the second floor.

"One of this author's specialties is roast turkey ..."

"I'm liking her already," I interrupted.

"I figured you would," Jillian said, returning the smile. "There's a turkey defrosting in one of the café's sinks. It should be thawed by now. The bird is too big for poor Shannon to handle, so I was hoping you'd be able to remove the giblets and rinse it out for her?"

I'm sure my face said it all.

"Oh, come now, Zachary. You've watched me prepare turkey. It's not that bad. I know that you know what to do."

"The things I do for love," I muttered, as I handed the dogs' leashes over.

Shannon is one of Jillian's newer employees, but she's a whiz in the café. She's made everything in those display cases from scratch: pastries, scones, muffins, cakes, tarts, and so on. However, Shannon is also less than five feet tall and couldn't weigh more than ninety pounds.

I won't bother describing how revolting it was, removing the bag containing the turkey's heart, gizzard, liver, and neck. Surely, the poultry industry could come up with a suitable alternative for those who will *never* use the Jeffrey Dahmer gift bag found inside the bird. Why don't they offer a frozen turkey that either comes *with* or *without*?

Back downstairs, I wasn't too surprised to find the dogs had attracted yet another crowd of admirers. I really shouldn't act too amazed. Those dogs were essentially the town celebrities, seeing how they were most recently thanked by the good Queen of England herself. Sydney was right. The dogs were a human interest story. Everyone wanted to meet them and absolutely everyone wanted to take their pics.

"Jeez, how long was I up there?" I laughingly complained, as I watched the steady string of fans shuffling past the corgis. Heck, I've actually been to the Louvre in Paris, and the efficiency of the line moving past the dogs reminded me of the line of people waiting to see the Mona Lisa. Actually, if you want to know the truth, the line in the Louvre moved faster. "Are you two ready to go home yet? We need to … well, this is new. They're wandering off? Jillian, could you grab those leashes before they make good with their escape?"

Both dogs were reeled in to an abrupt halt. Sherlock

looked back at me and gave me an exasperated snort. Watson uttered a low whine.

"The door is the *other* way, guys," I said, as I pointed to the front of the store. "There's nothing back that way but the storage room and the back cashier's station. Why do you want to go back there?"

Now Sherlock whined and both corgis tugged on their leashes. Sighing, I pulled out my phone once more and took another set of pictures in the direction the dogs were looking. Once more, the dogs were mollified, turned in place, and started for the door.

Kissing Jillian goodbye as we passed her, I started reviewing the events of the past couple of days. Ruby has started spouting lines and phrases that she couldn't possibly have heard from anywhere in my house. The dogs were now randomly staring at things, and once a photograph was taken, they lost interest.

Take all those things into consideration and I can only come to one conclusion: the dogs have taken a case, but they sure as heck didn't clear it with me. I have no idea what they're looking at. Perhaps it was time to check in with Vance? Maybe something was going on locally, and the dogs had picked up on it?

Yes, it was a long shot, but it was worth investigating. Either that, or the dogs were going to drive me nuts. As for Ruby? I actually cringe at the thought of what else that little parrot could be saying. I mean, come on. Virgins? Seriously?

"We have a stop to make," I announced, after I loaded the dogs and got behind the wheel of my Jeep. "We're going to go talk to Vance and see if there's anything happening in PV that we need to know about."

Twenty minutes later, we were walking through the Pomme Valley police department, only progress was slow. Just like Jillian's store, the place was filled with ardent admirers of the dogs, which is surprising, considering how my two corgis are responsible for solving more cases than the entire police department combined. Then again, in their defense, not much actually happens around here.

"If it isn't Sherlock and Watson!" one female officer cried, as she squatted down to give the dogs a friendly pat as we passed. "Aren't you two the bravest, smartest doggies in the whole world?"

Naturally, the dogs were loving it. I couldn't take more than a few steps before both dogs would drop to the ground and roll over. It got so bad with Sherlock that I inadvertently ended up dragging him—upside down—across the linoleum floor. Not far, mind you, but enough to make everyone around me laugh and then jokingly accuse me of pet abuse.

"Good afternoon, Mr. Anderson," a gruff voice said, from behind me.

"Oh, hey Chief Nelson. How are you today?"

"No missing murderers. No stolen loot to recover. I can't complain. Congrats on your wedding, by the way. Caught the ceremony with the missus at the school. You've got some powerful friends, Mr. Anderson."

"I have no idea how to respond to that."

The chief grinned and slapped a friendly hand on my back.

"Don't sweat it. I hear you went to Ireland for your honeymoon?"

"A self-driving exploration of the island, yes."

"That's precisely what my wife wants to do," the chief

admitted. "How was it?"

"Very memorable. If you've never been, then I can safely say it's worth every penny. Listen, if you ever do plan on making that trip, let me know, would you? I can give you some friendly pointers about what to do, what to pack, and more importantly, what *not* to do."

Chief Nelson nodded appreciatively before turning to look in the direction I was moving. "Are you here for Detective Samuelson?"

"I am."

"Is everything okay?"

I pointed at the dogs. "I personally think so, but it's odd. They keep acting like they're working a case, so I wanted to check in with Vance, just to be certain."

"All's quiet in PV," the chief told me, as he turned away. "Just the way I like it."

I found Vance in his office, hunched over his desk and scribbling away on a full-sized yellow notepad. However, as I approached, I watched him frown, rip the sheet off the pad, crumble it, and toss it in the trash can. Based on the number of wadded up paper balls around and *in* the waste bin, whatever Vance was working on wasn't going well.

"Catch you at a bad time?"

Vance looked up, saw me, dropped his gaze to the dogs, and immediately fished his bag of doggie biscuits from his jacket pocket.

"Hey, Zack. Come on in. I could use the break. Well, if it isn't Sherlock and Watson, everyone's favorite corgi duo. How are you two doing today?"

Two corgi rears were planted on the floor as Vance held out the biscuits. Once the dogs were happily enjoying their treats, Vance looked over at me.

"Is something the matter? You look … troubled."

"Something is bothering me, yeah. What are you working on? Looks like you've been killing trees in here for quite some time."

Vance scowled as he returned to his chair. "I've been asked to give a speech during the next policeman's ball, and so help me, if you make that crack about policemen not having balls, then I'll personally toss you in the holding cell and throw away the key."

I snickered and tried to order my smile to go away. It didn't work.

"Ah, heard that once or twice, have you?"

"Every single day," Vance confirmed.

"So, umm, you're giving a speech, huh? Dare I ask for whom?"

"Chief Nelson, who else? The twisted son of a …"

My friend trailed off as several female officers wandered by, but not before stopping long enough to give each of the dogs a pat on the head.

"… biscuit eater is getting back at me for hearing me call him cheap."

"You called the chief *cheap*?" I asked, incredulous. "Why in the world would you want to call your boss a name like that?"

"Well, in my defense, I didn't know he could hear me, all right?"

I leaned forward to tap the yellow notepad, which was almost empty, by the way.

"So, how's it coming?"

"Horribly, thank you for asking. What do you need, Zack?"

"Is there anything happening in town?" I asked, unsure

how to structure the question. "I mean, anything bad?"

"Anything bad?" Vance repeated, as he frowned. "Are you looking for a case, pal?"

"Am I looking for one? No." I pointed at the dogs. "But, I *do* think they're working one, only they're doing it without me. I just wanted to see if anything was up."

"I hate to break it to you, but the town has been quiet lately. Let's try to keep it that way, shall we?"

"Oh, no you don't. You can't possibly blame me for any type of bad publicity. The dogs may stick their noses in places where they don't belong, but even you can't possibly tell me it isn't good for our little city."

"I concede the point," Vance reluctantly admitted. "To answer your question, no, there's nothing really happening that affects us."

"That stinks," I decided, as I sat back in my chair.

"What has the Dynamic Duo been doing that has you so riled up?" Vance wanted to know, as he gave up on his speech writing and pushed the notepad away.

"You and I both know how the dogs behave when they're working a case," I began.

Vance nodded, and made a motion with his hand for me to continue.

"Well, I've caught them staring at various things, and they won't leave them alone until I take a picture."

"Hmm."

"Hmm? Is that all you have?"

"And when you take a picture or two, they lose interest?"

"Almost immediately," I confirmed. "And, not just once, or twice, but three times now. I already have a parrot who's acting up. I don't need the dogs doing it, too."

"The Hanson parrot?" Vance asked.

"Yep. Ruby. She's started spewing gibberish, and I have no idea where she's picking it up from."

"Couldn't she have come up with it on her own?"

I shrugged. "I'd like to think so, but from what I've heard, these types of parrots will only repeat what they've heard. They won't speak on their own. I mean, come on. It's a bird, for crying out loud."

Vance leaned forward and a smile appeared on his face. "All right, you've piqued my interest. What has Ruby said?"

"I forget what the first line was about. Something about boundless seas. And just recently, she spit out something about virgins."

Vance's eyebrows lifted and his smile turned into a smirk. "Zack, if you're going to watch that smut of yours, make sure the bird isn't listening, okay?"

"Hardy ha, ha," I scowled. "She hasn't picked up any of this from me."

"Sherlock and Watson act like they're on a case," Vance muttered, sitting back in his chair, "and Ruby is quoting things she knows nothing about. Hmm."

"And *that* is why we're here. But, if you say there's nothing going on, then I'm just going to chalk this up to some weird …"

"Hold on," Vance interrupted, as his chair thumped back on the ground. "Stay there. Let me check something."

Vance hurried out of his office as I turned to look at the dogs. Sherlock was sitting, sphinxlike, at my feet while Watson stretched out in her Superman pose. My timid little girl was watching the people walk by and perked up whenever someone stopped outside Vance's office to offer the dogs a compliment.

"I thought I'd check with all the surrounding

communities," Vance reported, as he returned to his chair. "I thought for certain someone, somewhere, might have an explanation for what the dogs could be interested in, but I was wrong. I'm sorry, buddy, everything is about as quiet as it could get in these parts."

Shrugging, I started to get to my feet when something on the opposite wall caught my eye. Turning to see what I was looking at, Vance followed my gaze and grunted as he reached up to take the sheet of paper off his bulletin board. Studying it intently, he looked at me and shrugged.

"Oh, this. I'm sure this has nothing to do with us."

"What is it?" I wanted to know.

"Details about a bank heist in Roseburg."

"Roseburg is north of us, isn't it?"

"About a hundred miles, yeah."

"Can you tell me what happened?"

Vance grunted once and squinted at the paper.

"Dude, just put your glasses on. I know you wear 'em. You know that I know you wear 'em, so what's the problem?"

"Don't get old, pal," Vance grumbled, as he pulled a thin, wire-framed set of reading glasses from his desk drawer. "Okay, let's see. As I said before, there was a bank heist in Roseburg. It went ..."

"How long ago?" I interrupted.

"Three weeks. Now, it went bad. One person dead. The culprits ..."

"Who died?" I asked.

"Would you stop interrupting me? Now, let's see. The victim was a security guard. The culprits were never caught, and the cash they made off with was never recovered." My friend looked up at me with a suspicious look. "Well?

You're not going to ask?"

"I will if you don't say anything else," I said, with a grin. "What'd they make off with?

"The amount? Fine. Looks like the thieves made off with nearly three-quarters of a million dollars."

I whistled. "That's a lot of cash. And none has been recovered?"

"Not a penny. Come on. You can't possibly think there's some connection to PV, right? Zack, you're grasping at straws."

Just then, a girl holding a large floral arrangement wandered by. Both dogs immediately perked up and stared in the direction she had disappeared. And, for the record, I recognized the teenager. She was Hannah's young assistant in the floral shop. Why would the dogs care about flowers?

I glanced at my friend and saw that he had noticed the dogs' behavior, too. His eyes skimmed the busy room, full of people and conversation, and noticed a few of the desks had floral arrangements already on them. Then, he turned back to the dogs. Watson was still staring in the direction the girl had gone, and Sherlock was only moments away from tugging on his leash.

"Stay here," Vance ordered, as he rose to his feet. "I'll be right back. Hey, miss? Excuse me, you with the flowers!"

I couldn't see Vance, but I could hear him. He had caught up to the teenager and, if I heard correctly, was escorting her to his office. Gripping the leashes tightly in my hand, we waited for their arrival.

"I'm sorry, this won't take up any time at all," Vance was saying, as he and the girl rounded the corner. My detective friend had relieved the girl of the arrangement and was holding it as though he had found the Holy Grail.

"Sherlock? Watson? What do you think?'

"Oh, I didn't see them as I passed!" the young girl exclaimed, as she smiled at the dogs. "I love corgis. Oh, hello, Mr. Anderson."

"Always an afterthought," I chuckled. "How are you? Megan, isn't it?"

The girl nodded. "You have a good memory."

Sherlock had risen to his feet, which prompted Watson to do the same. Both dogs stared at the flowers, transfixed. Vance carefully moved the large vase from one side of the tiny office to the other. The dogs tracked the flowers the entire time.

I held out my hands. "I see what you're doing. Here, give me those. Why don't you grab that vase on the desk just over there?"

Vance nodded. He passed the large arrangement to me and picked up the vase that had two lilies in it.

"Hey!" a young officer protested.

"I'll give it right back," Vance promised.

The lilies were ignored. Megan was ignored. *We* were ignored. The corgis continued to watch the large collection of flowers and ignored everything else.

"Well, that answers that," Vance decided. He returned the lilies to their owner. My friend took the vase back from me and studied the flowers. A grin formed on my face and I didn't bother to hide it.

"Still think there isn't a link to Pomme Valley?" I asked.

Wordlessly, Vance nodded. He handed the flowers back to Megan and bade her thanks. As soon as the girl and the flowers had both disappeared, Vance turned to me and shook his head. Then, he looked down at the dogs.

"Okay, guys. You have me convinced."

I noticed one of the flowers had fallen to the ground. Stooping to retrieve the broken stem, I studied the vibrant red petals. Roses. The arrangement had nothing but roses in it. Roses? For Roseburg? How the heck did they know?

FOUR

How in the world did I let you talk me into doing this? I mean, I have a stack of paperwork a mile high sitting on my desk that is demanding my attention. I really shouldn't have walked out like that."

"What are you worried about?" I argued. "You said it yourself; there's nothing going on. And paperwork? You're seriously going to complain about not being able to do paperwork?"

Vance held up his hands. "Fine, you win. What do you want me to say, thanks?"

Two uneventful days had passed. Ruby hadn't thrown out any more obscure messages, but seeing how I've still caught the dogs staring at the occasional unusual item, I have to conclude that there *must* be a reason for it. So, I talked my detective friend into going on a road trip with me. I knew it was a long shot, and the Roseburg police pretty much made it clear that we were not welcome to poke our noses into places where they don't belong. However, I've come to trust my dogs, and neither one was willing to let the matter go. So, it was time to do a little bit of investigative snooping.

Approaching the outskirts of Roseburg, having passed the city of Green not ten minutes ago on I-5 north, we drove by the county fairgrounds on our right. Both dogs reared up on their seats in my Jeep to look out the window. I was in the process of reaching for my phone when they lost interest and settled back down. Eyeing Vance, who shrugged, we drove on.

Crossing over the South Umpqua River, we followed the signs leading to the downtown district. Intent on allowing Sherlock and Watson access to the bank where the heist took place, both Vance and I thought there might be something which would catch the corgis' attention. After all, those two little dogs have discovered quite a bit, even when working with much less.

"How big is this town?" I asked, as we pulled into the bank's parking lot.

"Umm, I think they have a population over twenty-thousand," Vance reported.

"Larger than PV, but much smaller than Medford. That's even smaller than Grants Pass," I said.

I knew it was a mistake to try our luck at the bank when, as I carefully lifted both dogs to the ground, Sherlock took one look at the surrounding area and whined to be returned to my Jeep. And Watson? She was looking at me as though she suspected I really didn't have a clue as to what I was doing. Then again, let's face it. Coming up here was a long shot, but at least the two of us had already said those exact words.

I tried to get the dogs to walk with me up to the bank lobby's front door, but neither dog was interested. Sherlock, I could tell, was moment's away from slamming on the brakes. Watson noticed her packmate had stopped walking and immediately sat down.

"Come on, guys," I grumbled. "We just want your opinion on this place."

Vance appeared next to me and chuckled. "I think we were just given it." At my blank expression, he chuckled. "Look at them. They think this is a waste of time. Come on, there's no point for us to go in there."

"You're that certain?" I asked.

Vance nodded. "You aren't? They're your dogs, pal. You should know 'em better than that."

Spinning on my heel and taking a step back toward my Jeep had both dogs on their feet and pulling on their leashes, eager to leave.

"Tell me how you really feel, guys. Well, what now?"

Once we were seated in my car, Vance pulled out his notebook. "Let's see. Oh, here we go. I say we go talk to one Maynard Carter."

"Who's he?" I asked.

"He was the other security guard on duty at the bank."

"Well, why isn't he there now?" I wanted to know.

"I was told he retired," Vance said, as he flipped a few pages. "Getting robbed at gunpoint, and having your coworker murdered, is probably a pretty good incentive to either retire or find another line of work."

I started up my Jeep. "Where are we headed?"

Vance punched the address into his phone and automatically reached for my charger cable, which would connect his phone to my stereo. The Jeep's display lit up and, just like that, I was looking at a highlighted map, showing me the exact route to this former guard's house.

Where in the world was this technology ten years ago? Do you have any idea how helpful it could've made my life? I've been lost in so many cities that … whoops. I'm sorry 'bout that. I'll save that rant for a later date.

Maynard Carter was a quiet, easy-going guy who looked to be a little younger than me. When he met us at the door, I could see he was probably four or five inches shorter than me, and I was an even six feet tall. His hair was brown, like mine, and also like mine, it was graying. Thankfully, I can say that he had more gray in his hair than I do. His hands had minor callouses, suggesting he might not have been a security guard for too long. This guy was retiring? I hope he had something else lined up.

"Thanks for meeting with us," Vance was saying, as Maynard led us into his house. "I know this is short notice, and I'm sure you've already told your story to the cops over and over …"

"… which I have," Maynard confirmed.

Vance nodded. "Right. If you wouldn't mind, could you tell my companion and me what happened?"

Maynard shrugged. "I s'pose. What's with the dogs?"

I looked down at Sherlock and Watson. Neither appeared too interested in anything. Shrugging, I gave Maynard a sheepish smile.

"Oh, I don't know. Moral support?"

The corgis slid into down positions and were content to watch us bipeds have a friendly conversation.

"So," Vance began, "you're retired?"

Maynard fixed my friend with an incredulous stare. "Wouldn't you be, too, if all that crap happened to you?"

"I heard a person was killed," I chimed in, adopting a serious tone. "Was it one of the bank robbers?"

This time, I felt Vance's eyes boring into mine. When I saw that Maynard had looked away, I glanced at my friend.

"*What are you doing?*" Vance mouthed.

"*I'm trying to get him to talk,*" I mouthed back.

After a couple of minutes had passed, Maynard finally responded.

"It was a bad day for a lot of people," the former security guard sighed. "None more so than poor Chet."

Out of the corner of my eye, I saw Vance pull out his notebook.

"That'd be one Chet Sampson?"

Maynard nodded. "That's right."

"Did you know him well?" I asked, being extra careful to keep my voice free of emotion.

"Not well. But, that doesn't mean he deserved what he got. He didn't have to die. Those gunmen had what they came for. There was absolutely no need to get that violent."

"Meaning, they had the money?" Vance said.

Maynard nodded.

"What else can you tell us about them?" I asked.

"I couldn't see their faces, so not much, I'm afraid. They were wearing ski masks."

"Any guesses on their heights?" Vance asked, keeping his tone light. "Were they heavyset? Skinny?"

Our new friend fell silent as he considered. "Nothing really stood out. Lemme think. Wait. Skinny, but just one of 'em.'"

"Skinny," Vance repeated, as he jotted down notes. "I was told there were two of them. Is that right?"

"Yeah, that's right."

"Remember anything else about the skinny guy?" Vance asked, without looking up.

"Short. I can't believe I forgot about that until just now. I remember thinking that dude was short."

Vance looked up. "You're sure?"

Maynard nodded. "Mm-hmm. I remember thinking that he probably drove some jacked-up truck."

"Small man syndrome," I chuckled. "Everyone knows someone like that."

"Its technical name is the Napoleon Complex," Vance corrected. "What about the second guy, Maynard? Anything stand out?"

"He was taller, but not by much. I'd say he was at least six inches shorter than me."

"And how tall are you?" I wanted to know.

"Six-one."

"Making him about five-seven," Vance calculated. "Out of curiosity, the first guy. What do you think? Five-five?"

Maynard let out a snort. "No way. More like five-two, maybe even five-one."

"What about ethnicity?" Vance asked.

"I didn't see their faces," Maynard insisted.

"Did both of them speak?" I asked.

Surprised, Maynard looked at me and slowly nodded.

"Any foreign accents?" I asked. "Or, maybe one of them used a southern accent?"

Bemused, Vance fell silent as he waited, pen poised over paper, for Maynard to answer.

"Taller guy? No, not really. Sounded like you and me."

"But the other guy?" Vance hopefully asked. "You noticed something, didn't you?"

"It was the way he pronounced certain words," Maynard recalled, closing his eyes. "I'm trying to think of … jail cell, that's it."

"He said jail cell with an accent?" Vance asked, frowning.

"No, he and his pal were arguing, and I heard him say he didn't want to get thrown behind bars, only …"

"Bars came out like bahs, didn't it?" I guessed.

Suddenly, Maynard was smiling. "Yes! Exactly!"

Vance studied my face. "Well?"

"New England accent," I reported. "I heard it when I was in Maine. Bar Harbor, to be precise, only the locals called it *Bah Hahbuh*."

Vance added the observation to his notes.

"So, what does that tell us?" I asked.

Vance shrugged. "That at least one of these guys isn't from around here."

"Do you think they could be hiding in Pomme Valley?" I asked.

My detective friend pointed at the dogs. "You tell me. Your dogs are the two canine wonders here. You told me that they've been zeroing in on various items. What do *you* think?"

"I think anything is possible," I conceded. "I just don't know how Ruby ties in to this."

"Maybe she doesn't," Vance argued.

"Who's Ruby?" Maynard asked. "There weren't any women involved. Their faces might've been masked, but I would've known had one of them been female."

"No, umm, Ruby is a gray parrot," I explained.

"And you think a bird is involved in this?" Maynard asked, without bothering to keep the sarcasm out of his voice.

"Ruby has been repeating some strange phrases," I said, by way of explanation. "She didn't hear those things from me."

"So, your parrot started repeating these phrases?" Maynard asked.

"Yeah, and I have no idea what it means."

"Ask him what the phrases were," Vance chortled.

"What about the phrases?"

I leveled a stern glare at Vance. "Jerk. He relishes the notion of me constantly referencing something Ruby said about … virgins."

"Virgins?" Maynard repeated, as he tried—and failed—to prevent the smile from appearing on his face. "You don't say."

"He *does* say," Vance laughed.

"The both of you can bite me," I grumbled, but not before giving Maynard a lopsided grin.

"Well, if you ever figure out how virgins tie in with that bank heist," Maynard began, "you be sure to tell me, you hear? Just don't look for me at the bank. As I told you earlier, I'm now retired. When something that bad happens, and you're spared? It's a sign from above, tellin' you to find something else to do."

Maynard showed us to the door. He stooped to pat each of the dogs on the head as we walked past.

"Where to now? I asked.

Behind me, the front door to Maynard's house was just about closed when it opened back up.

"You know, you ought to talk to Officer Stanley Ogden."

The four of us—yes, dogs included—turned to look back at the former guard.

"We were under the impression we weren't welcome at the police department," I said.

Maynard's brow furrowed. "What? Why wouldn't someone be welcome at the police station?"

I sighed and indicated the dogs. "Well, it might have something to do with how popular these two are becoming."

"Sherlock and Watson," Maynard muttered, to himself. "Yeah, that's where I heard those names. The dog detectives. Weren't they in the news for finding some lost Irish jewelry?"

I nodded. "Yep."

Vance hooked a thumb at me. "*He* just got married last month at Westminster Abbey, in London. Not only that, the Queen of England was in attendance."

"The Queen and a couple corgis," Maynard reflected. "Makes sense. Oh, I get it. She was probably thanking you for solving that Irish mystery, huh?"

Again, I pointed at the dogs. "You mean, she wanted to thank *them*, but yes, that was the main reason."

Maynard squatted down, next to the dogs. I also couldn't help but notice his knees sounded a lot like mine: *snap, crack,* and another *snap.*

"Don't you worry about the police 'round here," Maynard told the dogs. "Maybe you could teach them a thing or two? After all, they haven't recovered the stolen money yet, have they?"

"The captain made it very clear he didn't want to see us," Vance reported. "We tried to get them to just send us a few files, so we could go over the basics of the case, but once they found out who we were, they clammed up and said they don't use consultants."

"Officer Stanley is a nice kid," Maynard told us, as he pulled out his phone "He and my son are good friends. I'll let him know you're coming."

* * *

The Roseburg police station was a hive of activity. One would think that a full-blown riot was happening somewhere in the city, but no. Apparently, this particular station was heavy into the community outreach program, so as a result, there was a steady stream of people filing in and out of the station. To complete the scene of a small-town police department, a troop of high school students had set up several tables in the plaza outside the RPD's main entrance, and were selling a wide variety of baked goods.

"Did Maynard say whether or not this Officer Stanley person is going to be meeting us outside?" I quietly asked.

A family walked by. The two kids, ages somewhere around five and six, noticed the dogs looking at them as they passed in front of the Jeep. Both kids tried pulling their parents to a stop, but neither parent noticed, which resulted in both kids being practically pulled off their feet. Protesting loudly as they stopped in front of the students' bake sale, the parents selected a few things before moving off. Both were completely oblivious to their kids.

"I don't care what Maynard or Officer Stanley says," Vance was saying. "If we show our faces in there, then we run the risk of stepping on some toes, and let me tell you,

Chief Nelson is not about to risk doing anything of the sort."

"That means we ought to wait out here, doesn't it?" I surmised. "Hey, that's fine with me. I was thinking we could … where are you going?"

Vance had unbuckled his seat belt and was just stepping out of the car.

"Let's face it, buddy. You are way more recognizable than I am. I can probably step inside there, ask for Officer Stanley, and step out without anyone knowing who I am."

"Please," I scoffed. "I could do the same thing. It's *those two* who are instantly recognized nowadays. I'm not a police officer or a detective. I'm the one who should go inside and see about …"

A group of four police officers approached us and nodded their heads. All four, I might add, looked to be in their twenties, plus, they were split right down the middle: two guys, and two girls. One of the young women, as she was passing the Jeep, glanced inside and saw the dogs. She came to an immediate stop as she looked at my two corgis, and then at me. A look of recognition appeared on her face.

I held up my hands in a pleading manner. "Now, don't go …"

"It's Sherlock and Watson!" the female officer practically cried. "From Pomme Valley! Look! They're right here! And here's Mr. Anderson!"

Sighing, and forcing myself not to roll my eyes, I glanced over at Vance. My good friend had such a smug look on his face that, if we hadn't been parked in front of a police station, I would have thumped him on the arm. Hard.

"Is it really them?" the other female officer asked.

"It looks like them," one of the male officers said. "Sherlock? Watson? Is that you? See? Look how they're jumping up and down! It's them!"

"Yep, thanks for getting them worked up like that," I joked.

"Mr. Anderson!" the first male cop exclaimed. He stepped forward and clasped my hand. "It's a pleasure, sir. You're here, at our station. Is there something we can do for you?"

"I don't suppose you could keep it down, could you?" I asked, as I lowered my voice. "We were told your captain is not a fan of the dogs, and we don't want to step on any toes."

"You're working a case?" one of the female cops asked, unable to mask her excitement. "Can we help? I'd love to be able to say I helped work a case that the famous Sherlock and Watson were on."

"We're still trying to figure that part out," Vance finally said. "Detective Vance Samuelson, Pomme Valley PD. Listen, we were told to ask for Officer Stanley Ogden. Is he working today?"

"Officer Ogden?" the second male said, speaking his first words to us. "Yes, he's on duty until four p.m." I watched his gaze drop down to the dogs and linger there for a few moments. "Guys? Don't you think this is the perfect way to cheer Stan up?"

"Cheer him up?" I repeated. "Does this have to do with that bank heist?"

"Is that why you're here?" the first male cop asked. "Although, I can't say I blame you. We couldn't find anything to investigate. The culprits fled in a stolen car, which was found later completely torched, the money was never recovered, and the two perps vanished. I think a couple of new eyes on the case would be just what the doctor ordered."

"Or noses," one of the female cops added.

"Stanley was a close friend of the guard who was killed," the first male cop explained. "He's been in a funk, and if we can't snap him out of it, then ... I think he's gonna quit the force."

"And your captain?" I asked.

All of them, and I mean both guys and both girls, checked their watches.

"He'll be at lunch," one of the girls said.

"He always has lunch at Tony's," the other one added. "I'd say you have about twenty minutes. Come on."

I tugged on the dogs' leashes to get their attention. "Sherlock? Watson? Your wish is granted. We're going to head inside and meet some more admirers."

The dogs, I might add, must've sensed what we were about to do and were quite ready to head inside. Sighing, and hoping we would be long gone from here before the irritable captain could return, Vance and I followed our new friends.

Once inside, we were directed to head down the hall on the left, entering a large, open area where there were at least eight desks arranged in a square. It must have been a busy day for Roseburg, because only three were occupied, and of those three, only one had a detainee sitting next to the police officer. In this case, it looked to be a young woman in her twenties. However, she had either been living a hard life, or else she had just woken up with one mother of a hangover, 'cause her hair was disheveled and matted; her clothes looked to be several sizes too big and were close to becoming rags.

Sherlock and Watson hesitated as we went to pass the desk. The officer seated before the computer nodded his head at us and returned his attention to the girl.

"Where are you from?"

"Milwaukee."

"Wisconsin? What are you doing all the way over here?" the cop wanted to know.

"Wanted to go 'xplorin', I guess," the girl admitted, albeit reluctantly. I could see she was clutching something to her chest, and whatever it was, the dogs seem to be drawn to it. "Aww, aren't you two cute?"

Looked like the girl had just noticed the dogs.

I tugged on their leashes. "Come on, guys. These two aren't here for you, all right?"

The dogs refused to be budged.

"What's with you two? Let's go!"

Sherlock and Watson's previous fixations came to mind. Was there something I should be paying attention to? And, of course, the simple answer to that was a resounding *yes*, but naturally, I wouldn't figure it out for a while. Waiting for the girl to look in another direction, I quickly snapped a picture. Right on cue, both dogs rose to their feet and hurried after the four police officers we had met outside.

Officer Stanley Ogden was tall, at six feet five inches, and probably didn't weigh more than one hundred fifty pounds soaking wet. I'd say he was one of those lucky guys who could eat anything they wanted, and thanks to their high metabolism, it wouldn't add a single unwanted pound on their frame. Lucky punk. Anyway, he had sandy brown hair, cut short in a military style buzz cut, and from the way he was slouching at his desk, I could tell he wasn't having a good day.

Apparently, neither dog felt like sneaking up on the poor guy, and decided to give themselves a thorough shaking once they arrived at his desk. Surprised, Officer Stanley looked up at the small group of people surrounding his cubicle and tilted his head.

"Hey, what's up? Did I miss something?"

The four police officers from our welcoming committee nodded wordlessly at me and hurriedly left. Looking over at Vance, who inclined his head in an attempt to let me start talking first, I held out a hand.

"Zack Anderson, of Pomme Valley. This is Detective Vance Samuelson, also of PV. And before they bark and shatter a few windows, we also have Sherlock and Watson down there."

At the mention of my dogs' names, Officer Stanley perked up. He rose to his feet and leaned over his desk to study the two canines who now had to seriously crane their necks to look up at the newcomer. After a few moments, the lanky police officer took my hand and gave it a shake. After he did the same to Vance, he returned to his seat, prompting the two of us to take our seats, too.

"What is a winery owner and a PV detective doing here? Oh, sorry. That's not the way to start a conversation. Hello, Officer Stanley Ogden, Roseburg Police. And yes, I know who you two are. Oh, wait. Let me guess. You two are here to investigate the bank heist? Did Captain Webber reach out to PV for help? Weird. That's so unlike him."

"No, he most certainly did not reach out to us," Vance confirmed. He offered the Roseburg cop a sheepish smile. "To tell you the honest truth, we aren't supposed to be here, and certainly not inside your station."

Officer Stanley grinned at this. "Ah. The captain doesn't know you're here. None of you. Got it. So, are these the two wonder dogs I keep hearing so much about?"

"I don't know about wonder dogs," I said, shrugging, "but they certainly are developing quite a large fan base. Sherlock is the one with black in his coat, and the red and white one is Watson."

Officer Stanley gripped a corner of his desk and, seeing how he was seated on a wheeled office chair, pulled himself around to the front, so he could see the dogs. Both corgis were wiggling with excitement, as though the world's biggest bag of doggie treats had just been placed on the desk.

"Hey, you two. Are you friendly?"

Both corgis dropped to the ground and rolled over, eliciting a snort of laughter from our new friend.

"Yeah, I'd say that's a big 10-4. So, if my captain didn't reach out to yours, then what are you doing here?"

I pointed at the dogs. "Long story short, they act like they're working on a case. There's nothing happening in PV right now, and when the dogs nudged us toward Roseburg, we found out that a bank heist happened here several weeks ago. Do you think you could tell us about it?"

Officer Stanley shrugged, sighed, and sat back in his chair. "I had no idea bank robbers were like that. Maybe I've watched a few too many movies? I don't know."

Vance's notebook appeared in his hand. "I know this was traumatic for you. Your fellow officers told us you were friends with the guard who was killed that day?"

Stanley nodded. "Chet, yeah. God, what a day. You're a detective? Have you ever come across someone so evil that you think they actually *enjoy* causing others misery and pain?"

"They were cold and ruthless," I guessed.

"More than that. They were … wild? Yeah, let's go with that. They were wild, like … like …"

"They were on something," Vance finished, after Stanley trailed off.

"That's my guess," Stanley said, nodding. "Remorseless, scary, and wild-eyed. Those are *not* qualities you want to find in an armed bank robber."

"What happened to Chet?"

"The thieves went after a lady," Stanley reported, falling glum. "They wanted her jewelry, which she gave them. Then, they pointed at her wedding ring. The lady said it was her grandmother's, and it couldn't be replaced. She begged them not to take it. Now, if possible, I'd say this just egged them on."

"They tried to take it, and Chet stepped in to offer his help," I said, nodding. "The poor guy."

"You've been to see Maynard Carter? He told us the skinny dude pulled a snub-nosed revolver and drilled him, right between the eyes. Maynard also said that was when the second guy, the taller one, came to his senses. A little. He said that they had to go, seeing how they could hear sirens approaching."

"How fast would you say they got here?" Vance asked.

Officer Stanley looked at Vance. "What's that? How fast *who* got here? Oh, you mean the police? The bank this happened at is only a short walk away. We didn't even know anything was wrong until we heard the gunshot. We were there in just a few minutes. Why do you ask?"

"We were told the money was never recovered," Vance

said, as he glanced at his notes. "None at all? They never tried to spend any of it?"

Officer Stanley shook his head. "We arrived much too quickly for them. They fled south, on I-5. They temporarily lost us in the Medford area, but we caught up with them in Talent."

"How long were they on their own?" Vance asked. He was adding notes at a furious pace.

"From the time they lost us, in Medford, to the time we found them again and managed to disable their vehicle with spike strips, only about thirty to forty minutes."

"Their car was disabled, yet they still got away," Vance mused. "Let me guess. They commandeered another car?"

"At gun point, yes," Stanley confirmed. "Here's the kicker. We have cell phone footage of the two guys stealing a second car, but they weren't carrying anything. No bags, nothing."

"They had stashed the money," I guessed.

Stanley nodded. "That's what we figured, too. Then, since there were so many cars present, we made the difficult decision to let them go. We couldn't endanger anyone else's lives. But, just because we let them go, it doesn't mean we still aren't looking for them. Medford PD has been contacted, and is actively helping us search for them. Their pictures have been circulated with everyone in the area, so it's only a matter of time before they're apprehended."

"I certainly hope you're the one who gets to make the collar," I told Stanley. "In Chet's honor, these two need to be put away for good."

"In Chet's honor," Stanley repeated, turning grim, "I hope they put up a fight. They need to be put in the ground."

We thanked Officer Stanley for his time, but suddenly, a commotion sounded in the direction we needed to go. Our four friends from earlier were laughing and joking, using very loud voices, mind you, as they were following an older gentleman wearing a dark gray suit with a black tie. He was of average height, around five feet ten, had unkept, unnaturally dark black hair, and a thick gray mustache. From the way the four officers were fawning over him, this *had* to be the captain. Oh, so that's why they were all practically shouting. They were alerting us, letting us know the captain was back!

"Oh, it's time to go," I whispered.

A look of alarm appeared on Vance's face. "It's the captain, isn't it? He's back?"

"Quick, you guys," Officer Stanley urged, becoming more animated by the second. "Step into interrogation room two. Hurry!"

The four of us, including the dogs, darted in the room. Stanley closed the door just as the captain passed by. A few pleasantries were heard. The captain asked how Stanley was handling his friend's death. Surprisingly, the officer said he was doing a bit better today, and was looking forward to finding the two thieves. Once the captain had passed, the door was quietly opened, and Stanley beckoned for us to follow.

"Do me a favor," Stanley said, as we quietly made our way to the station's front entrance. He handed Vance a business card. "If you find these guys down in PV, would you let me know? I'd like to personally be there when they're taken down."

Vance held out a hand. "As soon as we know something, we'll let you know."

Once we were back in my Jeep, the two of us burst out laughing.

"I haven't snuck around like that since I was in high school," Vance chuckled.

"Same," I added. "Too bad we didn't really learn anything that could help us."

Vance turned to me, incredulous. "Are you kidding? We got exactly what we needed: a possible tie to PV!"

"What? How?"

"Zack, think about it. These two thieves led the local cops on a high-speed chase down I-5. They made it as far as Medford, but they lost them there. Then, for nearly forty minutes, these guys were unaccounted for. I think that's more than enough time for them to put in an appearance in PV."

I held out a hand and waited until Vance passed me Officer Stanley's card. Entering his information into my phone, I handed it back. Vance shrugged, and did the same.

"You're saying we should assume they're hiding in PV?"

"Whether it's them, or the cash," Vance was saying, as he pulled out his phone, "this case has been dropped in our laps. I say we solve it!"

FIVE

It has often been said, by family, friends, and even me, that when I'm busy working on something, WWIII could happen, and I more than likely wouldn't even notice. When I'm writing? It's even worse. I can lose huge chunks of the day at one sitting. There are times when the only thing that can pull me out of whatever world I'm in is the pain my body begins to feel when sitting in one place for too long. Or my bladder, I suppose.

The point I'm trying to make here is when an author is fully immersed in his zone, then the last thing he wants to do is to leave. Words are flowing, characters are speaking, and activities are happening all around. For me, on this particular day, I was so far immersed into my zone that not even a ringing telephone could've yanked me back to reality. I know, since when I finally did emerge, my phone said three different people tried to reach me.

Today, my little slice of Oregon was overcast, the temp was hovering around fifty degrees Fahrenheit, and the skies were threatening to soak the locals with up to three-quarters of an inch of rain. I was sitting in my upstairs office, a can of Coke Zero Sugar was sitting within reach, and I was off in La La Land. Well, in this case, another country, if you must know. Scotland, or more specifically, Inverness. For those who have visited, you'll know that area is known by a much more romanticized moniker: the Highlands. Encouraged by my recent success at trying something new, I'd decided to start a new series based in the Highlands of Scotland, with a villain so evil you couldn't help but love to hate him. Of course, it couldn't hurt that my Count Goran character was nearly six and a half feet tall, more ripped than Thor himself, and could turn any woman's head. He had …

Sorry. I got carried away there. It's not often I write a book based on the antagonist's point-of-view, and I'm finding I really enjoy changing up the writing style like this. My agent, once she heard what I was proposing to do, couldn't give me the green light fast enough, which was a relief. I really didn't want to go looking for someone else to publish this story. My publisher, MCU, which I jokingly refer to *Man Chests United*, has been incredibly good to me, so I'm thankful they trust me enough to purchase whatever stories I come up with. This one? Well, I have high hopes I might hit the *New York Times* best sellers list again.

Anxious to do the country proud by incorporating everything I could remember seeing when I was there, I threw myself into my work. I wanted to include the numerous rolling hills, the lush green fields, and the narrow, single lane roads the locals affectionately think of as a freeway. Then, of course, I couldn't forget to include the fluffy highland cattle that looked like a cross between a teddy bear and a regular cow.

As long as I was looking for landmarks worth mentioning from Scotland, I would be remiss if I left out the most famous. In this case, I remembered stopping by the side of the road, gazing out at a quiet expanse of water, and being told this was the famous Loch Ness, and if I stared long enough that maybe—just maybe—I might be able to see Nessie for myself. There were no sightings for me, however, but I did enjoy the knowing that *this* was where the rumors started.

Describing the landscape, throwing in a mention of the fluffy local cows, and wondering how to tie in the famous Loch Ness, I could easily see how I almost missed what was about to happen. After all, if *their* room hadn't been just down the hall, then I might not have heard them. Sherlock, though, had the timing down. I had just finished describing how Count Goran's rolling estate included nearly three miles of riverfront access and was home to a wide variety of native fish, and the sadistic son of a gun would charge the village townsfolk to …

Woof.

Did a dog just bark? If they did, then I should be able to hear them. After all, they're just down the hall from me, in their own room. And yes, don't judge me. No one uses that room but the dogs. I have a nice, comfy couch set up, a clean bowl of water, and a 55" high-definition television in there, tuned to a channel specifically designed to keep animals entertained.

Yeah, I know. I know what you're thinking. But, let's face it. I've already heard them all. I'm nuts. I've finally lost all my marbles. I'm a few sandwiches short of a picnic. However, there comes a time when you're desperate enough to find something to occupy your pet's time that you'll try anything: chewy toys, stuffed Kongs, and their favorite squeaker toys. Well, one day, I found something new: a free preview for an honest-to-goodness pet channel, much like how the big studios will give away a free weekend of HBO.

Wanting to see for myself what type of content could possibly attract an animal's attention—and keep it—I decided to take a look. For the record, Sherlock and Watson were in the room with me. So, as soon as the channel began playing their program, I looked over at the corgis, intent on seeing for myself just how inaccurate their advertising could be. Well, imagine my surprise when I saw both Sherlock and Watson watching the program as closely as when they are watching me fill their food bowls. What type of program was it? Dogs chasing squirrels.

I remember tiptoeing out of the room and checking on them an hour later. There they were, reclining on the couch, enjoying their program. The show had changed to some documentary about butterflies, and on the screen was this gorgeous Monarch butterfly flittering from flower to flower. Both dogs were watching the show as closely as if I was checking out one of the new Star Wars shows.

I signed up for a year right on the spot.

Back to the present. I thought I had heard a dog bark, but seeing how I knew the television was on, I passed it off to one of their shows. A wait of a few more minutes confirmed I was either right, or I was off my rocker and imagined the whole episode. Whatever. Back to Scotland.

With Count Goran controlling the village's fishing rights, he could ...

Woof.

My head snapped up. All right, there was no doubt about it. Someone just woofed, and I was willing to bet it was Sherlock. It wasn't a loud bark, designed to get my attention as quickly as possible. Instead, it was more of a *hey, that's interesting* kind of bark. So, what had set him off?

Pushing away from my desk, I headed toward the dogs' room. The television was still on, but the pet station's streaming service must've locked up, because I was looking at the home screen. Activating the television app, and then selecting the pet station, I turned to the dogs. The program started. This time, I could hear some type of bird chirping, only the problem was, the volume was set fairly low. Plus, the program hadn't even been playing when I walked in, so that definitely ruled out the TV as being the source of the woof.

Both dogs were staring at me from their positions on the sofa, as though I alone was interrupting their day.

"All right, who barked?"

Both dogs blinked a few times as they watched me.

"Sherlock? Is everything all right? Watson? You're doing good?"

My little female rose to her feet, stretched her back, then melodramatically flopped over, as though the sheer effort of her shake had drained her of energy. Moments, later, she was asleep. Nodding, I turned to Sherlock.

"Roger that. So, you must be the one who woofed. What is it? Is everything okay?"

When Sherlock glanced back at the screen, I shrugged, and turned to go.

"Awwwooooowoooowoooo!"

Foot raised, about to take a step, I paused. Slowly turning, I looked at my tri-colored boy and grinned. Three syllables. Sherlock was definitely trying to tell me something.

"All right, you wanted my attention, boy. Well, you've got it. What's going on?"

Sherlock was still in a down position, in what I tend to call the sphinx position. He was watching me with a look on his face that said I was a complete dunderhead for not having figured out what he was trying to tell me.

"Don't look at me like that. Could we please lose the condescending looks and just skip to the part where you indicate what the problem is?"

Sherlock blinked his eyes as he stared at me. Finally, after a brief staring match, my little boy twisted his head around until he was able to glance down at his back. I swear to you, it was the first time I noticed he had his rider with him today.

"Hey there, Ruby. I didn't see you there. Are you … you're asleep, Sherlock? I have no idea why you brought me in here to show me Ruby." I leaned forward to scratch the affectionate dog on the top of his head. "She's asleep, so why don't we …?"

"1 … 5 … 8 … 5 … 2 … 1 … 5 … 9 … 2."

I stared at the bird and damned if I didn't stoop even lower, so as to get my ear as close as possible to the little parrot. After passing several minutes in an awkward silence, I was rewarded with the little bird suddenly fidgeting in place, as if she couldn't get comfortable. Her head slowly appeared from underneath her wing, but her eyes remained closed. Then, I heard it again:

"158521592."

If that wasn't a code, then I didn't know what was. Ruby must have mentioned the code once before, and Sherlock was alerting me to it by bringing me into the room. What a smart little dog!

"Good job, boy," I praised, ruffling Sherlock's fur. "You guys get extra treats tonight."

Quickly, before I could forget the number, I texted the code to the last person I sent a message to on my phone, which, of course, was my wife. Jillian promptly texted back.

IF THAT'S SOMEONE'S PHONE #, YOU'RE MISSING A FEW DIGITS.

I sent her a smiley face and told her it was just a number I didn't want to forget. Studying the sleeping bird for a few more moments, I straightened and gave my two dogs a speculative look. Where in the world could Ruby have picked up that particular number? Here's a weird thought: do birds dream? Whatever the case may be, I didn't think this was just some random number. It *had* to mean something, but what?

Looking at the cell in my hand, I started wondering who I could run my theories by. Vance? Yes, he was a detective, but he's a *working* detective. I can't keep monopolizing his time by approaching him with every conspiracy theory my wacko mind could come up with. Harry? He was a working man, too. This time of year is typically busy for him, so I really didn't want to bug him, either. Who did that leave?

Making up my mind, I dialed the number.

"Zachary! Is everything okay? You sent me that strange number and I was starting to wonder if you even knew you had sent it."

I laughed out loud. "You're insinuating I *butt texted* you?

Huh. That's a new one."

"Do you know who sent you that number?" Jillian asked.

"I do, yes, but unfortunately, she wasn't very helpful in telling me what it means."

In the few seconds of silence that passed, I somehow got the impression that Jillian was suddenly paying a little bit more attention to the conversation.

"Ruby said it, didn't she?"

"Yes, and before you ask, no, I haven't a clue as to what it means."

"I think we should talk about it tonight, over dinner."

"You're on, my dear. Should we invite the gang?"

"You might be able to get Tori and Vance," Jillian said, "but I know Julie won't be able to go. The twins have several doctor's appointments late this afternoon, so she and Harry are going to be tied up."

"Phooey. All right, I'll see if Vance and Tori would like to go. What place are we hitting tonight?

"I was thinking Marauder's Grill."

Visuals of a large, circular grill so overladen with meat that it had been known to lure the fiercest vegan back to the dark side, sprang to mind. And, if I wasn't mistaken, I started to drool.

"You're smiling, aren't you?" Jillian correctly guessed.

"Like you wouldn't believe. You have my vote, my dear."

"Wonderful. Will you reach out to Vance and Tori?"

"I'm calling him right now. See you shortly?"

"Count on it, Zachary. Love you!"

"Love you, too."

Yes, it was sappy, and I'm sure we sounded like love-struck teenagers, but do you know what? I didn't care. The two of us were incredibly happy with one another, and we weren't ashamed to let our affection show. Especially when certain friends tried to compete with me in order to make themselves look that much better with their significant others.

"Hey, Zack, what's up, pal?"

"Marauder's Grill tonight, at six. Can you and Tori make it? I've got another message from Ruby I think you'll want to hear about."

"You want to meet at Marauder's? Try and stop me, pal. We'll be there. Can't wait to hear what your bird said this time."

"It's just numbers."

The line fell silent. I had to check to make sure Vance hadn't hung up. And, for the record, he hadn't.

"What was that?"

"Numbers, buddy. Ruby spat out some numbers, and I'm hoping that, together, the four of us will be able to figure out what they mean."

"Harry and Julie not coming?"

"Jillian says they're going to be tied up."

"Ah, it's their loss. Marauder's. It's been too long. I think I'm gonna get a steak so big it'll put the one from the Great Outdoors to shame."

"The ninety-six ouncer?" I chuckled. "Yeah, I'd like to see that happen. No, wait. No, I don't."

"See you at six, buddy," Vance promised.

Later that night, after the four of us were seated at one of the restaurant's four—count 'em, four—dining tables, Vance pulled out his always-present notebook and asked me what the number was. Having long forgotten what

Ruby had said, I pulled out my cell and read it off.

"158521592."

Vance finished scribbling the number into his notebook and fell silent as he studied it. After a while, he glanced up at me.

"I don't suppose you can save us all some time and tell us what this means, can you?"

I shrugged. "No clue, amigo."

"What about your dogs?" Vance asked. "Have they given you any indication what it could mean?"

"The only thing Sherlock did was let me know Ruby was saying something."

Vance perked up at this. "Oh, really? I see what you mean. That number has to mean something. The question is, *what?*"

I noticed both Tori and Jillian had pulled out their cells. Both, it would seem, had the same intention in mind.

"Find anything?" I asked, after a few minutes of silence had passed.

Jillian shook her head and conceded defeat. "I only found some obscure reference to something on Walmart's website."

We all looked at Tori.

"I didn't have any luck, either. The only thing I found was a link to some obituary in Georgia. I spent the last several minutes trying to figure out why it showed up in my search results."

Jillian lifted her hand. "I did the same."

The two friends looked at each other. "You didn't find anything, did you?" Tori asked.

Jillian shook her head again. "Not a thing, I'm afraid. 158521592. Let's think about this. We know it's not a phone number."

"It's not latitude and longitude, is it?" I asked.

Tori shook her head. "Not unless they've secretly changed the rules. Latitude is a number that is less than 90, usually written out in degrees, minutes, and seconds. And longitude? It's a number that won't exceed 180."

"Well, scratch that idea," I groaned.

Jillian patted my hand. "It was a good guess."

Tori suddenly looked at my wife. "What about numerology? Could some type of formula be applied to it?"

"I don't even know what that is," I confessed. "Oh, don't get me wrong, I've heard the term before. But, as to what numerology means, I haven't a clue."

Vance nodded. "Ditto, pal."

Jillian returned to her phone. "Let's see. Here we go. Numerology is a pseudoscientific belief in a divine or mystical relationship between a number and some type of coinciding event."

"Pseudoscientific?" I scoffed. "That's all I need to hear. It sounds like it ranks right up there with astrology."

"That's what I'm thinking, too," Tori agreed.

Jillian raised her hand a second time. "All in favor of ruling out numerology?"

The four of us lifted our hands high into the air. All of us, I should point out, were holding our drinks.

"The motion is carried," Jillian announced.

"Let it be stricken from the record," I added, using a thick Scottish accent and rolling the *r* in the two words that had them.

Vance came close to snotting his beer. The waitress arrived with our orders at that time and expertly handed them out. She even included a round of refills, all without us asking about them. That, alone, will always get you a higher tip in my book.

We ate in silence for a few moments before Jillian took a drink from her glass of iced tea and dabbed the corners of her mouth with her napkin.

"I say we need to figure out where Ruby is hearing these messages."

The rest of us fell silent.

"Think about it," Jillian urged. "We already know Ruby didn't come up with these sayings on her own. That means that she, along with every other speaking parrot out there, overheard it from somewhere and decided to mimic what she heard. So, my question is, where did she learn it?"

All eyes turned to me.

"Hey, don't look at me. I have no idea where she picked them up, either."

"She's your bird, buddy," Vance pointed out.

"Yeah, I know she is," I complained, "but that doesn't mean I know where she picked it up."

"Have you taken her anywhere in the last week?" Tori asked.

I shrugged. "Well, yeah, I took her to Harry's office for a checkup after the first two comments."

"But nowhere before that?" Vance asked. He was looking down, at his notebook, as he scribbled notes.

"No, not at all. Ruby likes to hang around me whenever I'm home, and the last week or so, I've been home a lot."

"You're working on a book?" Vance asked, as he continued to write.

"I am," I confirmed.

Gone were the days that Vance used to chide me for

my primary profession. No more giggles, or scoffs, or rolling of his eyes when references to my being a romance author would surface, thank you very much. Ever since the book he asked me to write on his wife's behalf blew up the charts, earning us both a pretty penny and a steady royalty check, I had one super-supportive friend who was proud to announce my profession to anyone within earshot.

"How acute are a parrot's aural faculties?" Jillian asked.

"How cute is a parrot's *what*?" Vance asked, frowning.

"How sharp is a parrot's sense of hearing?" Tori translated.

"For example, if the source of these sounds are, let's say, a quarter of a mile away, would Ruby be able to hear it?"

I held up my hands in a helpless manner. "No idea."

"What about frequencies?" Tori asked, as she leaned forward in her chair. "Could she be picking up some type of signal, like a police scanner?"

My three companions turned to me again. Once more, I was holding up my hands, as if at gunpoint.

"Not a clue, guys. Do I look like an ornithologist to you?"

"Like a *what*?" Vance asked. His frown was back, and it was bigger than before.

"A bird expert," Jillian explained.

"Oh. What's with the big words, guys? Are y'all trying to make me feel like a bumbling idiot?"

"Sorry," I apologized.

"Not you," Vance said, waving me off. "You're a writer. I'm talking about you two. We already know you're both smarter than me. Try not to make it too obvious, 'kay?"

Tori giggled. "Then, don't make it too easy."

"Hill-arious," Vance said, shaking his head. "So, is there any merit to this? Should we be getting an ortho … orzo … bird expert on the phone?"

Surprisingly, Jillian nodded. "That's a great idea, and I know just the person to call. Here we go. Let me dial the number …"

We all watched—transfixed—as my wife tapped in a number on her cell phone, placed it on the table, and hit *dial*. After a few moments, we heard the number start to ring.

"Hey, Jillian. What's up, chica?"

I knew that voice anywhere, seeing how it belonged to my best friend. I should've been the one to suggest calling Harry. After all, he *is* the town veterinarian. He probably knows enough about birds to be able to answer our questions.

"We're sorry to bother you, Harry, but we have a couple of questions about birds. First, though, how are the twins?"

"A handful. They might be a little over six months, but they're starting to crawl. How is it possible for them to move so fast? Kids. So, hey everyone! Wish we were there with you. Who's on the phone?"

As we all leaned forward to wish Harry and Julie the best, I quietly placed a mobile order on my phone, and arranged to have it delivered to my friend's house. I could hear it in his voice: he was exhausted. It was early enough in the evening to know that neither he nor Julie would have had time to make dinner yet. Let it be a surprise for them.

After everyone had said hello, I slid Jillian's phone closer and took a breath.

"Harry? Do you have time for a couple of quick questions?"

"Sure. Fire away, bro. The answers are: never would have imagined it, what the heck were we thinking, and I'm getting way too old for this."

I couldn't help it. "I'll take … What do I think about becoming a father to *two* babies at the same time, please, Alex?"

My friend sighed loudly. "You can kiss sleeping goodbye. Oh, to be able to have a solid four nights of sleep again."

I looked at Jillian and mouthed *four?* She nodded and held a finger to her lips. Then, as an afterthought, she reached over to a nearby table and confiscated one of their menus. Before she could open it, I laid a hand on hers and shook my head.

"It's been taken care of, my dear."

My wife's face lit up with a huge smile before she slipped her arm through mine. Together, we looked back down at the active call on Jillian's phone.

"So, listen," I began, "could you possibly tell us how good a bird's hearing is? Like Ruby, for instance. How far away would she be able to pick something up?"

"For a parrot? Gosh, bro, they can hear, obviously, but it's nothing out of the ordinary. Let me think. A typical parrot can hear a range of frequencies between 200 Hz to 8.5 kHz. The ability to hear is nowhere near as important as their eyesight. Is this still about the mimicry Ruby is doing?"

"That's right, pal. We were all just wondering how close would the source have to be in order for Ruby to hear it and to start mimicking it?"

"It'd have to be fairly close," Harry decided. "Take us, for example. Our sense of hearing is better than theirs."

"No way," Vance declared.

"You heard me say the range for parrots? Well, a human typically ranges from 30 Hz to nearly 20 kHz. It's a much wider range of frequencies than for us humans."

"Scratch that theory," I groaned.

"Think they had super-human hearing and could hear something from miles away?" Harry laughed.

"It might've been brought up," I admitted. "All right, what about those frequencies? Any chance a bird could pick something up, like a police scanner?"

"Seriously, bro? Can you? The answer is *no*."

I held up my hands. "Well, I'm zero for two."

My wife suddenly sat up straight in her chair. "Zero for two."

"What is it?" I wanted to know. "Did you figure something out?"

"What was the number again?"

Vance consulted his notes. "158521592. I'm with Zack, here. I haven't a clue what it could mean. But, I also know *you*, Jillian. Did you figure something out?"

"158521592," Jillian repeated. "Or, that could be read as … 1585 to 1592?"

"Didn't you just say the same thing?" Vance asked.

"No. The two in the middle? What if it wasn't a number *two* but the word *to*?"

Tori gasped. "Ruby was stating a range of years! *This* to *that*. How clever!"

Vance added another line of scribble to his notes. "1585 to 1592. All right, it looks good on paper. What does that tell us?"

"It tells me," Harry's voice began, "that we're missing out on all the fun, bro. Not cool!"

"You sound tired, Harry."

"Tired? Oh, no. I'm not tired, I'm beat. Pooped. Barely keep my eyes open, yet ..."

"... there's so much to do?" I finished for my friend.

"Exactly, bro. I meant what I said earlier. I'm getting too old for this."

"I feel for you," I said, raising my voice. "We all do. Tell you what. Dinner is on me tonight."

"That's nice of you, Zack, but we're okay. We just have to find something easy to fix and then we ..."

"It's taken care of," I interrupted. "It'll be there in about twenty minutes."

"Uhhhh, you ..."

"... are welcome," I finished. "You guys enjoy it. Thanks for your help. We'll keep you in the loop, buddy."

Glancing over at Jillian, I saw her nodding appreciatively at me. Vance leaned forward and caught my eye.

"You bought them dinner? When?"

"About five minutes ago."

"What? How? You didn't say anything."

I held up my phone. "I didn't have to. I ordered them some food from here and arranged to have it delivered to their house."

"I need to learn how to use my phone," Vance complained.

"I've been trying to teach you," Tori said, as she shook her head. "My student, unfortunately, clams up every time the subject is brought up."

Vance smiled sheepishly and plucked the dessert menu from the holder at the table. Jillian, I could tell, had returned to her phone and started a new search. While my wife tapped away on her phone, I noticed Vance drop the menu he was holding and turn back to me.

"What?"

"I take it you saw last month's royalty check?"

I should, seeing how I'm the one who arranged for the Samuelsons to split the proceeds with me, but there was no point in bringing up that particular tidbit here, at the table.

"I did, yes. It was a monster, and you will never hear me complain about getting a check like that in the mail. Wait. Didn't you?"

"Oh, no worries, buddy. We got it."

Tori placed a hand over mine. "You have no idea how much you've changed our lives."

"Oh, don't tell him that," Vance groaned. "His head is already big enough."

Tori's eyes sparkled with amusement. "So, I suppose I shouldn't tell him who reached out to me to thank me for inspiring such a wonderful story?"

Curious, I turned to Vance. "Oh? This is news to me. Who?"

"We're never gonna hear the end of this," Vance muttered. But … at least I can say there was a smile on his face.

"Selena Gomez."

I looked at Jillian for clarification, but finding her staring at her phone, I looked at Tori. "Isn't she a singer?"

Tori nodded. "She's done some acting, too."

"All right. She reached out to you guys? How cool!"

"Apparently, both she and her mom are huge fans of the book," Tori said. "Ms. Gomez was hoping there was a sequel in the works?"

"I'll have to think about it," I confessed. "*Heart of Éire* was written as a stand-alone novel, and I'm not sure where else I could take the story. Vance? You're developing one heck of a …"

"Don't say it," Vance grumped.

"Oh, the girls love it!" Tori gushed. She looked at us and grinned. "They're all fans of her music. They're thrilled to death that Ms. Gomez has personally reached out."

"Well, I'll be."

Conversation at our table immediately dropped off. Collectively, we all turned to Jillian.

"These numbers? We're right. It's a span of years."

"Whose years?" Tori wanted to know.

"You're never going to believe this. Guys? 1585 to 1592 are known as William Shakespeare's Lost Years!"

SIX

The following day found me parking my Jeep outside of PV's most popular book store: A Lazy Afternoon. This particular store used to belong to Pomme Valley's own femme fatale, Ms. Clara Hanson. She was also the former owner of Ruby the parrot, but seeing how the unfortunate Ms. Hanson was no longer with us, and her daughter, Dottie, really didn't care for birds, Ruby ended up with me. I should also point out that the reason I was getting ready to step inside the bookstore had nothing to do with my newest pet, but more of … all right, it kinda did, but right now? I wanted to learn more about William Shakespeare.

For whatever reason, Ruby seems to be spouting out random quotes and facts about England's most famous playwright, and I'd like to know why. The last clue, about the span of time known as Shakespeare's Lost Years? It *had* to mean something, but what? Well, that's why I was here: to pick up a book about the world's most famous writer.

Yeah, I know what you must be thinking. Why not just look up what I need from the internet? Well, the answer to that is, I could. However, I wanted something tangible, something ... concrete, I suppose, and in my mind's eye, that was an actual physical book.

Now I hear you arguing I should be headed to the library. After all, there will be many more resources available there than here, and yes, those were all physical books, too. Well, yes, that is true, and I guess the only response I have to that is I wanted to check on Dottie. Clara Hanson's only child has become part of our extended family, although that certainly wasn't because of anything Jillian or I had done. Quite the opposite. Dottie had arrived in town and kinda inserted herself into our lives. Long story short, the young lady was simply lonely, and in her eyes, Jillian and I had become parental figures. So, like a father would do, I kept an eye on her, just to make sure she was okay.

"Zack!" Dottie exclaimed, as soon as Sherlock, Watson, and I walked through the door. She had been sitting on a stool behind the counter, poring over some type of shipping printout, when she hurried over to give me a hug. Dottie Hanson was in her mid-twenties, had shoulder-length blond hair (with streaks of purple, green, and blue in it), and was dressed in faded jeans with a swirly tie-dyed shirt. She had three or four studded earrings in each ear, and was also wearing a tiny gold loop in her nose. No, not the kind that would remind you of a cow, but the other, more tasteful type of nasal piercing. "It's good to see you! What brings you here today? Uh, oh. It's not about Ruby, is it? I told you before, yes, she was my mom's parrot, but no, I can't take her. Ruby doesn't like me."

"It's not about Ruby," I assured her. "Sherlock? Watson? Leave her alone, okay? She's not here to play with you."

Dottie reached under the counter and found the bag of dog treats every store seemed to have. "Would you two like a treat?"

Two corgi rears immediately sat.

"Here you go. So, you're not going to try and convince me to take Ruby? Oh, good."

"Well, I *am* here about Ruby, but it's not what you think."

"Huh? What's that supposed to mean?"

I laughed and shook my head. "Yeah, I know how this is going to sound, and there's no other way to say it, so I'll just tell you. You know how parrots can mimic what they hear, right?"

Dottie nodded. Her hair, pulled up in a high ponytail, bobbed up and down.

"Ruby has started quoting Shakespeare, and I'm trying to find out why."

Dottie was shaking her head.

"Well, I certainly didn't tell that crazy bird anything the last time I was at your place."

True. The last time she was at our place, Jillian and I introduced the clueless woman to the wonderful world of retro science fiction films, starting with the classic *Last Starfighter*. Thankfully, Dottie enjoyed the movie just as much as we did.

The shop owner took a couple of steps back and stared at me for a few moments before crossing her arms over her chest.

"All right, I'll admit I'm curious. What did Ruby say?"

I pulled out the tiny notebook I carry in my back pocket to jot down book ideas. Flipping it open, I started skimming the pages.

"Do you always carry around a notebook?" Dottie asked.

I shrugged. "I'm a writer. It only takes losing a really good idea for a book to start carrying around something to take notes. I promised myself, after losing the idea and being unable to bring it back, I'd start carrying around a way to jot those errant thoughts of mine down. In this case, Jillian and I looked up the two quotes Ruby has said, along with the years."

"Years? What years?"

"The last bit of random stuff Ruby said was a number," I explained. "158521592, which actually turned out to be 1585 *to* 1592. All three ramblings were about Shakespeare in some fashion."

"How can I help?" Dottie wanted to know. "What's the first quote?"

"My bounty is as boundless as the sea," I relayed. "And, for the record, Ruby was stuttering when she said it."

"Stuttering? How …?"

"On the b's. In this case, my b-b-bounty is as b-b-boundless as the sea. Get it?"

"Oh, okay. That's weird. I didn't know birds could stutter."

"They don't," I confirmed. "She only mimicked the stuttering because that's how she must've heard it."

"Wow. That's interesting! What's the second quote?"

I turned my notebook's page.

"Oh, you'll laugh at this one: *virginity breeds mite, much like a cheese.* Yes, before you ask, she stuttered on this one, too."

"Virginity breeds mites?" Dottie giggled. "Where in the world did she pick *that* up?"

"No clue, I'm afraid."

"What do they mean?" Dottie inquired.

I flipped back to the first quote. "The 'bounty is as boundless as the sea' quote? It's from *Romeo and Juliet*, and is spoken by Juliet."

Dottie leaned against the counter and her hands rested on her hips. "Huh."

"And the second?" I continued. "The virgin one? It's from Shakespeare's *All's Well That Ends Well*. I haven't looked up which character said it, but I do know William Shakespeare wrote it. That's two for two."

"And the years?" Dottie asked.

"1585 to 1592," I reported. I didn't need to read the years from the notebook, which were there, by the way, because I had said the range so many times they were inadvertently memorized. "Those years? They are known as something called the Lost Years of William Shakespeare."

Dottie was silent as she digested this latest bit of news.

"Now you see why I'm here," I said.

Surprisingly, Dottie was shaking her head. "No, I would have imagined you'd be at the library instead of here. That's where you go when you're doing research, you know. Aren't you a writer? You should know that."

A grin appeared on my face. Dottie playfully swatted my arm. Sherlock's head jerked up and he started watching Dottie like a hawk.

"Don't listen to me. I'm just teasing you. I'm glad you stopped by. It's been a little slow in here today, and I was looking for something to pick me up. You'll do just nicely."

I gave her a neck bow. "Why thank you, m'lady."

"Jillian's right. You're silly."

"Dost thou, or dost thou not, haveth anything in here to do-ith with yon William Shakespeare?" I asked, using my not-so-authentic impression of an English nobleman.

"That can't possibly be the right way to ask that in old English," Dottie giggled.

"Yeah, what can you do?" I grinned. "Whatcha got?"

"Well, I don't have much, but maybe this will work for you."

The dogs and I followed the girl through the many racks of books until we stopped at a section entitled Classic Literature. Dottie selected a heavy, leather-bound volume with gold lettering on the spine. She pulled the book free of its neighbors and handed it to me.

It was titled *The Complete Works of William Shakespeare*.

"You just happen to have one of these lying around?" I asked, as I thumbed through the delicate, thin pages.

"I don't anymore," Dottie reported. "I had two, and that's the last one."

I followed Dottie back to the cash register and waited as she rang up the book.

"I can only hope my books will continue to sell after I'm gone," I stated, as I signed my receipt, "even if it's only a fraction of the sales Shakespeare gets."

"Funny thing about that book," Dottie said, as she slid the book, in its bag, over to me, "is that your book is the second one I sold this week."

Bag in hand, I had taken several steps for the doors when what Dottie had said sunk in.

"Wait. In the last week, you sold another book like this?"

"The exact same one," Dottie said, nodding.

"How often do you make sales in the Classic Literature section?" I asked, being certain to keep the eagerness I was feeling out of my voice.

"Not often. It's one of those sections I wish I could do away with, only what kind of bookstore could I say I ran if I didn't have the classics?"

"So, uh, how long ago did the other book sell?"

"Oh, I don't know," Dottie answered. Her head was down and she was lifting the cash tray out of the register so that she could place the credit card slip underneath. "Last Friday?"

"Making it the day before Ruby started spouting her nonsense," I whispered to myself. Looking up, I checked for security cameras. Sadly, there were none. "Any chance you can tell me what this person looked like?"

Dottie finally looked up. She saw the eagerness I was unable to hide and she curiously cocked her head. "Well, it was a guy. Umm, nothing really stood out. Why would you care about him, Zack?"

Do I tell her about Roseburg's bank robbery, or don't I?

"The dogs are working a case, and I think Ruby's ramblings might be related. I'm trying to find out how—and *who*—she picked up those quotes from. Think, Dottie. Do you remember anything about him? I can't help but notice there aren't any cameras in here."

"No, no cameras, I'm afraid. That's a level of technology that is waaayyyy above and beyond what I can comprehend."

"And if I were to help you install it?" I asked.

It was Dottie's turn to shrug. "Well, then, I'd probably take you up on that. In fact, it looks like mom bought a security setup a while back, but never got around to having it installed. Can you really help me get it going? I'd be eternally grateful!"

"I can probably do it," I confirmed. "Jillian and I will be by this weekend, okay? We'll get you all taken care of."

"Thanks, Zack. I don't know what I'd do without you two. Oh! You asked about that guy who bought the other book? I just remembered something about him."

"What's that?" I wanted to know.

"Construction," Dottie answered. "He reminded me of a construction worker. It was probably the outfit: dirty blue coveralls, muddy work boots, and a bright orange vest."

"Sounds like someone who works in construction," I said, scratching my chin. "Is there anything else you can remember?"

"Only that … he didn't seem the type," Dottie reluctantly added. "I hear myself saying that and I cringe. I never would have imagined someone looking that scruffy would want to catch up on his Shakespeare. Is that important?"

"To be honest, Dottie, I don't know. But, I will jot that down. Maybe Vance could use it?"

Just then, I felt twin tugs on the leashes. The dogs were up and ready to go. Thanking Dottie for her time, I headed for the door, only to be brought to an immediate stop. The leashes went taut, but that's as far as they got. Neither dog, it would seem, was ready to leave.

"What are you two doing?" I asked. Gently tugging the leash, I tried again. "Guys? We have what we came for. We're leaving, so let's get going!"

Both dogs had wandered over to the largest, widest

display in the store and seated themselves before the offering of books, as though they were paying homage to the mighty Altar of Printed Material.

"What is it?" I asked, growing irritated. "We've been in here before. You guys have been in here before. What's the holdup?"

The rack in question was where Dottie displayed all her new releases: thrillers, mysteries, romance, and a selection of titles currently on the *New York Times* best seller's list. For that matter, I even saw a few of mine on that rack. Looking down at the corgis, I moved to the left and then to the right as I tried to triangulate on whatever had caught their attention. For the record, it seemed to be the top shelf, which had the newest of the new titles.

"They're books," I told the dogs. "It's not too surprising, based on our current location. Let's go, 'kay?"

Sure enough, neither dog budged. Watson looked back at me and whined. Sighing, I pulled out my cell, waggled it in front of the dogs, then took a few pictures.

"There. Happy?"

"Are they?" Dottie asked.

Sherlock and Watson navigated their way around the counter and various book racks on their way to the door.

"Apparently. This time around, it should be interesting once we get to deciphering the corgi clues. I have no idea how everything is going to tie together."

"Well, when you get to that part, let me know, would you?"

"You are cordially invited," I returned, earning a smile from the girl.

Back in my Jeep, we turned right on Main Street and headed toward home. I wanted some quiet time to skim through my newest purchase. Hopefully, something in there would stand out and help me figure out why someone chose to broadcast those strange messages, and, of course, how Ruby managed to hear them when I did not. After all, the little parrot has been a resident of my home for a while now, so the only way she would mimic those messages would be for her to hear them. In my home.

It just didn't make any sense. Speaking of making sense …

Sherlock and Watson stirred. Both had been stretched out, in my Jeep's backseat, as though they were truly enjoying the fact that they had their own chauffeur. Something, and I don't know what, had caught their attention, and now they were both vying for the best vantage point to see what was in front of us. Sherlock stepped forward, onto my arm rest, and stared—straight ahead—at the traffic in front of me.

"Woof!"

"Yeah, I heard you, pal. There's no need to …"

"Awwwwooooooo!" Sherlock howled.

"Okay, I gather you'd like to file a complaint against someone. It'd better not be me. What is it? What's gotten you two riled up?"

"Ooooo!" Watson added.

"I'm driving! What do you want me to do, get out my phone and snap a picture?"

Three blocks and five howls later, I angrily whipped out my cell and snapped several photographs. Almost immediately, both corgis settled down and sank back into their seats, acting like nothing had happened. What *had* happened? A few cars had passed us, yet they didn't seem to care. One car did end up cutting in front of me, which almost had me slamming on the brakes and catapulting both corgis through the windshield, but a quick course correction avoided that. I should point out that neither dog complained about my driving. So, what, then, were the dogs staring at?

The only other vehicles on the road, and it had to be a vehicle, seeing how they continued to howl at me for several more blocks earlier, was one of those new hybrid electric cars and a city bus. Both cars were ahead of me the entire time, and both, I might add, turned off on side streets after I snapped a few pictures. Anxious to get my mind off the crazy events that were happening around me, I turned on the radio. Thankfully, the three of us made it home without any further incidents.

Unlocking my front door and stepping inside brought all three of us to an immediate stop. It smelled *heavenly* in here! Jillian had to be cooking something, and whatever it was, it had me drooling just as much as the dogs, I'm sure.

"Does that smell good or what?" I commented, as the leashes were hung inside the front closet. "Jillian? Are you here? Hello? If you're a burglar, and you're willing to cook like that, then I'll personally give you a key to the place."

There was no answer.

Wandering into the kitchen, I saw right away something was in the oven. A quick peek inside had my mouth watering: it was a honey-glazed ham, one of Jillian's specialties. Taped to the front of the oven was a hand-written note:

DINNER IS STARTED. HANDS OFF, MISTER! LOVE YOU! J.

Wallet and keys were placed on the counter. Turning to the dogs, I grinned at them.

"I don't know what we did to deserve her, but I think you'll agree with me here when I say we're incredibly lucky to have her. Oh, for Pete's sake, now what's on your mind?"

Both dogs were staring, unblinking, at the oven.

"Seriously? It's just a ham. There's nothing in there to go gaga about. You guys know you don't get to have any ham. It's not good for you. Plus, we've had hams before. Why all this fixation now?"

I don't know why I bother asking rhetorical questions. It's not like I expect the dogs to answer. However, neither dog would budge from the middle of the kitchen. Curious, I pulled my phone and snapped a single picture. As if that one act broke the spell, both dogs rose to their feet, gave themselves a thorough shaking, and walked—together—into the living room. Both corgis jumped up, onto the couch, and stared at me, as though they were waiting for me to do something.

"What? Do you want to watch television? Only in your room, guys."

The dogs blinked at me.

"Okay, stop it. You're creeping me out a little. What about the radio? Would that help you calm down?"

Reaching for a remote, the receiver was turned on, an 80s station was selected, and music started playing.

"Enjoy the Bangles, guys. If you need me, I'll be upstairs."

Sherlock rolled over and fell asleep. Dogs.

Several hours later, I was upstairs, in my study, hard at work. How hard? I was reading. My new book, containing all the work William Shakespeare has ever written, was before me, propped open on my desk. I had already skimmed through *Romeo and Juliet*, *All's Well That Ends Well*, and half a dozen sonnets, when I threw in the proverbial towel. Whatever the motivation was for those strange quotes, I had no idea how they all tied together. Could it be they were just ramblings from one Shakespearean fan to another? Could this be nothing more than a wild goose chase? Or, more alarmingly, could I have misinterpreted this whole scenario? For all I knew, this could just be random mutterings from a parrot.

Thoughts of Sherlock and Watson came to mind. If these were just bits of random gibberish Ruby had overheard, why, then, were the dogs so interested? There was no mistaking what the corgis thought of this situation. Sherlock and Watson have been treating this whole ordeal like they're on a case. So … what do I do about it?

The answer came quickly enough: keep researching. My instincts were telling me that I was missing something, and until I figured it out, they weren't going to shut up. Taking a quick peek in the pet room to see if the dogs had followed me upstairs at some point, which they did, *and* finding Sherlock and Watson asleep, I left them alone with their pet station still playing on TV. Realizing I had some uninterrupted free time in front of me, I decided to pull out all the stops and see what sort of sleuthing I could do on the internet.

Deciding to ignore the lines from *Romeo and Juliet*, as well as *All's Well That Ends Well*, I centered my efforts on the long number. Could it be that we were wrong, and Ruby was repeating the number exactly as she had heard it? Several online searches proved I was, if you'll pardon the pun, barking up the wrong tree. There were no exact hits.

Just like Jillian and Tori, I received several strange results. One took me to Walmart's website and another to some obscure obituary from a newspaper in Georgia. Okay, scratch that idea. It was best to assume Jillian was right and that number was meant to depict a span of years.

1585 to 1592.

Up popped William Shakespeare's Lost Years. Again. Clicking on various links, the meaning of those years became clear. Apparently, in Shakespeare's life, there were two times when he went off the grid and practically disappeared from the history books. The first time was from 1578 to 1582. Then, the second was from 1585 to 1592. What Shakespeare was doing during those years, or where he was, cannot be proven. So, what do historians do when presented with such a dilemma?

They guess.

During the second set of years, many historians believe Shakespeare disappeared after the baptism of his children. Everyone's favorite dramatist didn't reappear until the early 1590s, when he popped up as a London-based playwright. I also learned that these historians are intrigued by Shakespeare's second set of lost years because this would be the time when he would have perfected his craft and established himself *as* the aforementioned dramatist. This would be the time in his life when he would gain the experience of the theater.

It wasn't until I moved to the ongoing theories did it become interesting. There were several theories about why Shakespeare disappeared the way he did. First up was thievery. I found an obscure reference to Shakespeare poaching something from a neighbor, and in order to avoid the neighbor's wrath—and presumably the authorities—

William fled.

A second theory was that Shakespeare might've made a pilgrimage. Where? To Rome, where he could have been seeking refuge from England's persecution of Catholics. If you were someone who practiced Catholicism during Elizabethan England, it would have been a very dangerous time, indeed. The question, and most historians agree they don't know, was William Shakespeare a practicing Catholic?

Again, no one knew for certain.

Pushing away from my desk, I rubbed my eyes. It certainly felt like I had not blinked once in the last two hours. Plus, my back chose this time to voice its displeasure of its recent treatment. Groaning like a senior citizen rising from a seated position, I stood up.

"Getting old sucks," I announced to the room.

As expected, the room didn't care.

Walking down the hall, I poked my head back into the pet room. The three of them were still asleep. And the TV? It was back to the home screen. Seriously, what was causing the program to lock up? Maybe I needed to update the firmware? Whatever the case may be, I wanted noise coming from the room, thereby making it easier for me to sneak around unnoticed. Once the screen was displaying another riveting video showcasing some type of animal doing who-knows-what, in this case, there was a border collie chasing sheep around a large paddock, I knew this particular service, this distraction, was worth every penny.

Don't knock the show. I can hear you laughing. Being someone who works from home, there are times when you *need* some distraction for your pets. This service provides exactly that: something for them to do. This way, neither of the dogs are underfoot and I can get some work done.

It's totally worth the ten dollars a month I pay for it.

Tip-toeing down the stairs, I kept circling around to the questions bouncing around in my head. What did Shakespeare's Lost Years have to do with the other two messages? How did the three of them all tie together? And why would a bird be repeating them? It could only mean that, somehow, Ruby was overhearing them, but how? And from where?

I only made it a dozen steps down the stairs when two sleek, furry forms zipped by me, going at least Mach 1. I caught a quick glimpse of a discoloration on Sherlock's back and knew that Ruby had been tagging along. They may have disappeared around the corner, but I could still hear them scrambling to make it into the kitchen as quickly as possible. Then again, I was halfway tempted to join them, seeing how wonderful the house smelled at the moment. I also heard someone moving around in there, so I can only assume Jillian made it home. Strange that I didn't notice her arrival. Catching up on my Shakespeare must've been more distracting than I would have believed.

"Is that you, Zachary?"

Walking around the corner, I nodded. "Guilty as charged. When did you make it back? I didn't hear you come in. Then again, neither did the dogs."

I gave her a quick kiss before she pulled me in for a hug. We stayed like that for a few moments, long enough to have me wondering if something was wrong.

"Are you all right?" I asked.

"Mm-hmm. I'm just really enjoying coming home to a house with you in it."

I smiled at my wife and made a play of scuffing my foot on the floor. "Aww, shucks, ma'am."

"How does the ham smell? Good? I hope so. I'm not happy with this particular brand's glaze, so I made my own."

"You made your own glaze?" I repeated, amazed. "Wow. There's not many people who can say that *and* be able to pull it off at the same time."

"It's not hard," Jillian said, as she tapped a button on the oven. The interior light flicked on. "You just have to get the right proportion of … you don't care, do you?"

"Not one bit," I confessed. "I trust you implicitly."

Just then, an overwhelming sense of alarm washed through me. Something was wrong, and I couldn't quite place it. Jillian noticed the expression on my face and immediately took my hand in hers.

"What is it? What's the matter?"

I slowly looked down at the floor. Both corgis were there, but neither were paying attention to us. In fact, Sherlock was staring at the oven, and Watson had positioned herself to look back, toward the living room. I watched them for a few moments and, after noticing neither were moving, turned to look at my significant other.

"Did either of them come up to you to say hello?"

Surprised, Jillian's eyes widened. "Come to think of it, no, they didn't. Neither of them did."

"When we made it back from Dottie's store," I recalled, as I slowly walked around my stationary dogs, "and stepped foot inside, both dogs headed in here and both, at the time, stared at the oven as though you were incubating a dragon egg."

"The ham *does* smells good," Jillian said. "I know they can smell it, so maybe …"

I held up my phone, which is what caused my wife to

trail off. "After I took a picture, both lost interest. Sound familiar?"

Jillian turned back to the oven. "Huh. I don't know what to make of that. What's Watson looking at?"

"I don't know. Something in the living room? Sherlock? We get it. You want a piece of ham, all right? Well, I'm sorry to say, it's not gonna happen. Pork isn't good for you. Watson? Is there something in there you want to show me?"

Watson casually got to her feet and trotted out of the kitchen. The three of us—and that included Sherlock, too—followed her to the living room where we watched her place herself before the entertainment center and sit down. After a few moments, Sherlock joined her. Together, the two of them stared up at the large wooden piece of furniture holding up my television and housing several electronic components.

"Sherlock is now doing the same thing?" Jillian asked. "What are they looking at?"

I'm sorry to say that I actually knelt down on the floor and lowered my head so that I could look up, in the same direction as the dogs. I realize I *may* have looked silly, but at least I figured out what had caught their attention.

"The electronics," I reported, as I regained my feet. "They seem to be staring at my receiver."

"Is that the radio you have playing?" Jillian suddenly asked.

"Yeah, I needed to clear my mind earlier. Thought it'd help distract me. Sorry. I don't normally put that on. It must be what the dogs are being drawn to."

"The radio ..." Jillian repeated, as she softly trailed off. She turned to look back, at the kitchen. She slowly turned to look down at the dogs and then dropped into a squat next to them. "Is that so? Well, aren't you the smartest doggies in the whole wide world?"

"What is it?" I asked, confused. "You're acting like you just figured something out."

Jillian nodded. "I think I did. Zachary, what was Sherlock staring at?"

"The oven," I answered.

"Yes, of course. What do I have in the oven right now?"

"Oh. Well, the ham, obviously."

Jillian pointed at Watson. "And what was she looking at just now?"

"My receiver," I answered.

"Which was doing what?"

I shrugged. "Umm playing the radio?"

"Exactly! Zachary, put those two together and what do you get?"

I looked back at the kitchen and then over at my receiver. Oh, holy crap on a cracker. I missed it! I couldn't believe I missed something so obvious!

"That's it! That's the answer! Ham radio!"

SEVEN

Two days had passed and I was still kicking myself over missing a simple, trivial detail like that. Ham radio. It was the missing clue that identified the source of Ruby's messages. However, it didn't answer the question of *how* my parrot was able to pick up those transmissions. After all, the frequencies are higher than anything either of us would be able to pick up, regardless of whether you're a human or a bird.

Since, admittedly, I know next to nothing about amateur radio enthusiasts, I took it upon myself to see what I could learn about one of America's more popular hobbies. Want to know the first thing I looked up? The appeal. Why were so many people getting their FCC licenses so they could operate their own radios? Well, once I read the answer, I understood. Amateur radio, or ham radio, brings together fellow enthusiasts, electronics, and communication. I learned that people used these radios to speak with other users across town, across the country, and even across the world. My eyebrows lifted when I learned they could even communicate with astronauts on the International Space Station.

Most people are familiar with police scanners, so it shouldn't be surprising to know that your scanners can also scan the more common frequencies that ham radios typically broadcast on. And there, in black and white, was definitive proof that there was no way Ruby was picking up these transmissions on her own. The most common frequencies used? That would be between 440 MHz to around 1296 MHz To give you some context, do you remember what Harry said a few days ago? About which frequencies a bird could hear? That was from 220 Hz to 8.5 kHz. Now, if you don't know what those letters after the numbers mean, I can tell you Hz is short for hertz. One hertz was the same as one cycle per second. So, that meant Ruby could hear sounds between 220 cycles per second up to around 8,500 cycles per second, hence the addition of the K. Now, those numbers for the ham radios? Note the M. Those frequencies are broadcast from between 440 *million* hertz up to 1296 million hertz. There was no way a small parrot was capable of hearing anything that high, let alone a human.

So, with that being said, were there other frequencies a ham radio might employ? Maybe something lower? A few more online searches came up with the answer, which was a resounding no. If anything, the frequencies went *up* instead of *down*. Certain bands of frequencies were reserved for certain functions: airlines, police, fire department, and so on. The ham radios could only operate on very specific frequencies, and to hammer home the importance of not tampering with any frequency you weren't supposed to, the FCC requires all active ham radio users to be licensed. For the record, that involves taking—and passing—a test.

It was definitely way too much trouble for me. I'll stick to my police scanner, thank you very much.

My police scanner! I haven't seen the crazy thing since I moved to PV several years ago. Could my old scanner be the cause of this? Could it be tucked away in a drawer and maybe, just maybe, it could have been jostled and accidentally turned on?

I began yanking open my desk drawers. If it was in here, then I was going to find it. And, I really *really* hoped I'd find it turned on. Maybe that was why Ruby hadn't come up with another message? The scanner's batteries had petered out and it was now nothing more than a hunk of plastic?

Time will tell. I *will* find that blasted thing and put this to bed once and for all.

A whopping fifteen minutes passed. Well, I could call off the search. Did I find it? Oh, yeah, right where I figured it would be: in a junk box. I found the box in a storage cabinet in my office's closet, and I can safely say, with one-hundred percent certainty, it *wasn't* responsible for Ruby's messages. This particular model ran off of six double-A batteries. The battery compartment employs the use of a large, white plastic bracket, which is what holds all the batteries in the proper orientation. The battery holder was found *outside* the scanner, and it was cracked. That scanner will need a new battery holder before it'll ever operate again, and based on the corrosion of the batteries, it hasn't been used since I lived in Arizona.

Restoring order to my office, I sat back in my chair and considered my options. I was sure I was on the right path, only I didn't have a clue where to go from here. What would really be helpful was if I could hear the message the same time Ruby did, but that would mean … ?

I sat up in my chair. If I wanted to hear one of these mystery messages to Ruby, then I was going to have to hang out *with* the flippin' parrot, on an extended basis. Only then would I be able to determine where the transmissions were coming from.

Pushing back from my desk, I hurried into the pet room. Sherlock and Watson were asleep on the couch. And Ruby? From the looks of things, the little parrot had made herself a nest on Sherlock's back and had made herself quite comfortable. But, she was awake, and she was watching me.

Tapping my shoulder, I called the bird to me, to which she obliged. Once the parrot was sitting on my shoulder, in proper pirate fashion, I decided to carry on with my day. After all, I did have things to do.

I barely felt the bird's presence as I returned to my study and finished researching ham radios. There wasn't too much more to do there, having learned everything I needed to learn about amateur radio, and that is … best leave it for those who enjoy it. The information I had gleaned from the internet confirmed my suspicions: Ruby didn't pick up those transmissions on her own. No, somehow, and this is the part that continues to bug me, that little parrot was using something *else* to listen in.

I spent the rest of the day with Ruby attached to my

shoulder. I wrote a few more chapters in my latest book. I cleaned up the kitchen from where I heated up some leftovers for lunch. Moving to the laundry, I ran a few loads of blankets and pet-related items through the washer.

As for Ruby? She was delighted with the attention. She kept nuzzling the side of my neck, which kept making me think I had a bug crawling on my skin. Believe you me, that's *not* something you want to feel. I almost swatted poor Ruby off her perch no less than five times. And, I swear the little stinker was enjoying watching me jump like I had stuck a finger in a light socket.

It wasn't until after lunch that I noticed a pattern with Lentari Cellars' only avian resident. Ruby would mimic a sound she's heard after hearing it at least three to four times. Now, I don't know if other parrots behave the same, only this is how mine was behaving. How do I know this? Well, let me set the scene.

After I had finished lunch, and the four of us—me, Ruby, Sherlock, and Watson—finished sharing a bag of fresh, uncooked carrot sticks, I got my first glimpse into how a bird's mind works. Jillian sent me a text, which had the effect of sounding like a cricket chirping. After a few back and forth responses, I started noticing the chirping, but nothing coming through on my phone.

"Is that you?" I asked the bird.

Ruby cackled and bobbed her head a few times.

"Make a different sound, would you?"

For the next hour or two, Ruby entertained herself by recreating the cricket chirp and watching me fumble for my phone. Glaring at the bird, I laid a finger on her beak and shook my head, which only made the gray parrot more excited.

Then, I received my third or fourth generic call on my cell, which meant someone who wasn't in my address book had called my number. It also meant my phone, based on how I have my ring tones configured, rang like an old-fashioned telephone. Well, Ruby learned that one, too. She nailed the pitch and length on her first try. Needless to say, that friggin' bird had me reaching for my cell all day. Trust me, it got old *fast*.

Knowing more about ham radios than I ever thought possible, and completely certain Ruby had somehow been eavesdropping on these messages, I called Jillian.

"Well, knowing what you do, what's the next step?"

"I believe I know what we have to do," I reported.

"You do?"

"I think it's time we gather everyone together and go over our corgi clues. We've got some smart people in the group. Someone, somehow, must be able to figure out where to turn next."

"I like that idea," my wife told me. "Where do you want to go?"

"Do you know what? Why don't we have it here? Let's face it. Next week? This house will be gone. One last hurrah for Aunt Bonnie's old house."

"I like it, Zachary. You're on. What should we order? Pizza?"

"Sarah's Pizza Parlor. Everyone loves it, plus, I heard somewhere that they've expanded their menu. I'll find it online and print it out."

The rumors were true. Pomme Valley's favorite pizza restaurant was now offering several different types of crusts, four new sauces, an array of burgers, and several choice sandwiches. Not really sure what we should try, I ordered a selection of just about everything and arranged to have it delivered this evening.

* * *

"Man, I am diggin' this thin crust," Harry announced, several hours later. "I mean, it's crunchy, flavorful, and … and … I don't know, man. Words don't do it justice."

"You're just happy that Julie is allowing you to have pizza," Vance said, eliciting grins from the rest of us.

"Too true, bro. Too true. I ain't arguin', neither."

"You *aren't* arguing, *either*," Jillian corrected, throwing Harry a disapproving frown.

"Sorry, Jillian. I know you're a stickler for proper English."

"You apologize to her and not to me?" Julie demanded. She may have sounded angry, but I knew she really wasn't. She, along with her husband, had jumped at the chance for a night out of the house. Granted, it took a team of professional, experienced babysitters to convince them to come, but once we told them we'd foot the bill, and the two ladies literally showed up with their resumés and a list of references, Harry and Julie couldn't get over here fast enough.

"Ham radios," Vance moaned, after I told him about the big reveal in the kitchen from a few days ago. "Of course that's how Ruby has been picking up those messages. I can't believe I didn't think of it earlier."

I held up a hand. "Just a moment. It still leaves one very important question: how in the world did a parrot pick up a scanner frequency?"

"Maybe it's a frequency they can hear?" Vance suggested.

It was now the end of the week, and our gang had

assembled for our weekly powwow, so to speak. Typically, we let each member of the group choose a restaurant to go to, only this time, since it's my turn, we decided to just meet here, at my house. What do we do when we're all together like this? Well, that's easy. Each week, our good friends like to get together and go over what happened to one another since the last time we hung out. It's a tradition we started last year, and am pleased to say that it has stuck with everyone. Who's everyone? Well, there's me, Jillian, Harry, Julie, Vance, and Tori. And lately, we've started including the youngest member of our group, and that's Dottie.

If you don't do something similar, then I would encourage you to start a gang of your own. Reach out to friends, or family, and just stay in contact with one another. It's a great way to learn about what's going on in your friends' lives, whether they're hurting, need help, or, perhaps, would like help celebrating some type of milestone? My only piece of advice is … don't wait too long to get started. You never know when someone you'd like to connect with will no longer be able to answer the phone.

"Harry already confirmed Ruby can't pick up anything in the Megahertz range," I said, as I placed an overloaded plate of food at the table and pulled out my chair. Jillian did the same next to me. "Admit it, Vance. The reason you didn't think of ham radio earlier is that, deep down, you knew it was impossible."

Vance pointed at me and nudged his wife on the shoulder. "There, you see that? That doesn't make me sound inept, or foolish. Let's go with his theory. And, you're right. I remember considering it once, but quickly ruled it out, figuring there'd be no way Ruby would be able to pick up one of those radio transmissions on her own."

"And therein lies the problem, I'm afraid," I said, sighing heavily. "We need to figure out how she's doing it. I spent the whole day with her, just to see if Ruby would be willing to lead me, or else show me, how she was doing it."

"I take it she didn't, bro," Harry commented.

"She didn't," I confirmed. "But, I did learn something important."

"What's that?" Jillian asked, looking up from her conversation with Tori and Julie.

How that woman could carry on a conversation with someone else, yet know to look over, or ask a question, at the appropriate time continues to elude me. She's amazing, she really is.

"In order for Ruby to repeat something, she needs to hear it at least three times."

Everyone turned to Harry.

"I didn't know that," Julie confessed. "Is that true?"

Harry shrugged. "They obviously only need to hear it once, but who can say if all birds behave the same? It's not like it's no ... I mean, it's not like there are rules that birds have to follow. Zack, you heard Ruby mimic something?"

I held up my phone. "She's got my text alert for Jillian down pat."

Jillian smiled. "You mean ... the cricket chirp?"

"The one and the same," I said. "And, it gets better. She has my phone's generic ring down, too. That crazy bird had me reaching for my phone all day."

A full plate of pizza, wings, breadsticks, and half a cheeseburger was placed next to mine. Dottie pulled out her chair and sat down. She saw everyone staring at her and she offered us all a sheepish smile.

"I skipped lunch. Zack? About the mimicking phone calls? Ruby used to do that to my mom, too."

Interested, I looked at the girl sitting next to me. "Oh?"

"I mean, I know me and Mom didn't really talk that much, but I found quite a few references to Ruby in her letters. Mom loved that bird, no doubt about it."

"Any word on whether or not you guys think the two bank robbers might be hiding in PV?" Tori asked.

"PV is connected to that case in some fashion," Vance insisted. "We just don't know how yet. Personally, I think they're here."

"Why not in Talent?" Jillian asked. "That's where they were last seen. What makes you think they'd come here?"

In response, Vance pointed at me. "Because, Sherlock and Watson think they are."

I was in the middle of taking a sip of my drink when Vance explained his reasoning. I ended up snorting my soda.

"The only thing I'll confirm is that their Royal Canineships have been paying attention to a lot of weird details." I held up my cell and waggled it. "Sooner or later, the corgi clues will start to make sense. The more eyes we have looking at these pictures, the better chance we have of figuring them out. I think that's the only way we're going to know whether or not PV is linked to the Roseburg bank heist."

"Could be the loot," Harry offered.

I held up my hands. "Only time will tell."

Jillian stood up and clinked her glass with her fork. Conversation immediately dropped off as all eyes turned to my wife.

"Thanks for coming, everyone. Tonight is symbolic, for

both me and Zack. We have an announcement to make."

"You're pregnant," Harry declared, before Jillian could take a breath.

"What? No, I'm not. We …"

"… are splitting up," Harry said, trying again. "Oomph! Jules! Why'd you do that?"

"They're not splitting up, you dope. Would they have all of us over if they were? Let her finish, would you?"

"No, we're not splitting up," I confirmed.

"Then, what is it this time?" Vance asked, as he set down the slice of pepperoni pizza he had been munching on.

Jillian looked at me and nodded her head to encourage me to take over. Standing up, I faced my friends and smiled.

"This will be the last time you guys are all invited to this house."

If it wasn't quiet before, it certainly was now. Deathly quiet. Seeing all eyes on me, I suddenly realized how that must've sounded.

"That didn't come out right. Let me try again. Tonight's the last time we're all going to have dinner in this house. This one, right here."

"You're moving?" Julie asked, dumbfounded.

"You're selling the winery?" Vance asked, shocked.

I looked at my wife. "It's official. I suck at this."

Jillian laid her hand over mine. "Let me try. Everyone? By this time next week, this house will be no more."

"You're tearing it down!" Tori guessed. "This is it, isn't it? This is where the two of you are going to live together?"

"In a house we designed ourselves," Jillian confirmed, nodding.

"Demo starts next week. I'm told the old house will

be gone in several days, and cleanup afterward will take an additional couple of days. All in all, construction is scheduled to commence in a couple of weeks."

"Where are you going to live until then?" Vance wanted to know. "Do you need a place to stay?"

Tori elbowed him in the gut. "Really? Where do you think he's going to stay, at a hotel? He'll be at Jillian's house while this one is being built."

"Oh. I forgot about Carnation Cottage. Sorry, guys."

"No worries," I told my friend.

Harry appeared on Jillian's right and placed his own heavy plate of food on the table. Julie eyed him, then the plate, and then shrugged. Blowing kisses to his wife, Harry picked up a piece of Hawaiian pizza and took a healthy bite.

"What're you doing with all this stuff in here?" Harry wanted to know.

I shrugged. "A few things have been set aside for a couple of people who expressed interest. Burt, from the antique store, was here not that long ago. He's taking so many things that he said he's gonna have to rent a bigger truck."

"How are you going to know how much to charge him?" Julie asked. "No, wait. I just heard how ridiculous that sounded. You're giving it all to him, aren't you?"

"This stuff was never mine to begin with," I explained. "It was all Aunt Bonnie's stuff. I only have a very few things in here that I plan on keeping, and they'll be going into storage. So, I'm okay with all of it going away."

Vance perked up. "Is there anything Burt didn't want?"

Tori leveled a glare at her husband. "What? We don't need anything else, thank you very much. Our own house is crowded enough as it is."

I waited for Vance to look my way before nodding. "As a matter of fact, there is. Believe it or not, he didn't want either the loveseat or the main couch. He said it wouldn't be worth the effort to sell it since it wasn't really his style. So, I'm contacting St. Vincent's to see if …"

I trailed off as I watched Tori and Vance both turn to look at the blue floral print loveseat and the (unmatching) beige sofa and regard the two pieces of furniture in utter silence.

"Vance? Tori? Do you guys want the couches?"

The two of them turned to look at each other.

"Are you thinking for the playroom?" Tori asked.

Vance nodded. "Loveseat in the playroom, and the couch in the garage."

"For your workout room," Tori said, nodding.

"You agree?" Vance asked, hopeful.

"Sure. That's fine."

I laid a hand on my wife's. "Dear, remind me to call St. Vincent's tomorrow and cancel the truck that's supposed to be here Monday morning."

"Of course, Zachary."

Vance rose to his feet, took his empty paper plate—and a few others—to the kitchen and threw them away. Sitting back at the table, he made a play of wiping his area clean with his napkin.

"You know, we're all here right now. Why don't you let us take a look at your pooch puzzles?"

"Corgi clues," I corrected, "and do you know what? That's a great idea. Would anyone have any objections to giving me and Vance a hand?"

Jillian pushed her drink away from her so that the area

in front of her was clear. "That sounds like a wonderful idea, Zachary. Surely, with all of us here, we should be able to figure out what Sherlock and Watson want us to do and how PV may be involved with this Roseburg case."

"I sure hope so," I added. "So, far, we're at an impasse. I'm hoping someone will be able to recognize something I haven't, and then point us in the right direction."

"Oooo, I remember doing this when you guys were working on my mom's case," Dottie exclaimed, from my left. "I can't get over how smart Sherlock and Watson are. I love your dogs, Zack."

"Everyone does," Jillian said.

Harry held out a hand. "Well? Gimme your phone, bro. I'll …"

"*Give me*," Jillian corrected, without looking up, "and you didn't even say please."

It was Julie's turn to thump her significant other in the stomach.

"Watch those manners, Harrison."

"Sorry, Jules. Zack? Would you please pass me your phone?"

"I've got a better idea, actually," I said. "Let the few of us who aren't finished eating do just that, and then we'll take this to the living room. I'll show you what I learned my phone can do. It's going to make things a lot easier for us tonight."

Jillian swatted my arm. "Showoff."

While we waited for the stragglers to finish eating, I brought everyone up to speed on the specifics of Roseburg's bank heist, which included what we knew, how much was at stake, and showed clips of the footage for those who wished to see it. Fifteen minutes later, we were all seated around the television in the living room. As soon as we were all settled, I reached for the remote.

"We're watchin' television?" Harry asked. "Cool! What're you puttin' on? A movie? Oomph. Jules, that's three times! Do you have to keep socking me in my gut?"

"You already know we're going to be helping Zack figure out the corgi clues. We're not watching TV right now, got it?"

"Actually, we are," I added, giving Harry a grin. "Kinda. Look at this. I can take my phone and mirror it to my television."

"Bull," Vance snorted. "In order to do that, you'd have to know what you're … huh. Get a load of that. How are you doing this, Zack?"

"Many of these new televisions now can speak *cell phone*. So, when I want to look at a video, or a picture, I'm essentially telling the phone to use *this* display, and not its own. It's called *casting*."

"Can all televisions do this?" Vance wanted to know.

"I'd say as long as the television is less than two years old, then there's a better-than-average chance it can. You just have to look, and make certain both the cell phone and the television are connected to the same wireless network. Okay, I've got my pictures loaded and am ready with the first. Everyone ready? Good. Here's the first."

An image of Main Street, with a number of visible vehicles, popped up on my TV.

"Looks like Main Street," Jillian observed.

"That's because it is," I recalled. "I don't know what set the dogs off. Sherlock started woofing and I couldn't see anything worth looking at around me, so I started taking pictures. Let me see. Yep. Pics two and three are of the same thing. Well, mostly. You can tell that I was driving."

"Which, as an officer of the law," Vance drawled, "I must say is a no-no. You're not supposed to be messing with your phone while driving."

"I know that," I returned, "and you know that. Plus, I've seen you send out texts while driving, too, so don't give me that."

Tori turned to Vance. "You told me you quit doing that."

Vance gave me an accusatory look.

"Hey, if you're taking me down, then I'm taking you down with me," I laughed.

Vance chuckled and shook his head. "Thanks a lot, pal. Hey, go back to the first pic, would you?"

Scrolling backwards, the first photograph reappeared. In it, we could see stores along the street, including Spencer's Toy Closet, and Wired Coffee & Café. Driving along the street were two sedans, one pickup truck, several commercial vehicles, and a bus.

"Do you see something?" I asked.

Vance squinted at the TV.

"Glasses, pal," I told my friend. "I've done as much as I could to get the picture as large as possible. If you still can't see it, then you should be wearing your glasses."

"Fine," Vance grumbled, as he pulled his glasses out. "Ah, there we go. Nope, I thought one of the cars looked familiar. It doesn't."

"Anyone else?" I asked the room. When no one said anything, I nodded. "Roger that, we're moving on. Here we have …"

"My store," Jillian finished for me. "The dogs fixated on something in Cookbook Nook? Any idea what?"

I stared at the picture. "It's just a picture of book racks, and a few displays, I think."

Jillian nodded. "That's right. I usually have two or three special promotions each week, in order to highlight an area that is underperforming."

Dottie stared at the screen and was nodding. "That's actually a brilliant idea."

"You sound so surprised," I laughed.

Dottie's face flushed red. "That's not what I meant. I'm sorry."

"We're just teasing you," I assured the girl. "And you're right, it's a fantastic idea. Dear? Are there displays in that direction?"

"I'm getting you some glasses, too," Jillian teased. "You can see two of the displays, although, I will admit they're small. The first? Do you see these little splotches of red on the right? Those are Dala horses. The display is Swedish-themed. Cookbooks, cast-iron pancake pans, and so on."

"Try the pepparkakor," I suggested. "If you like ginger snaps, you'll love those thin little cookies. Warning: if you get started, you won't stop until you hit dust."

"What about the other display?" Tori asked. "Where is it and what's it contain?"

"It's on the left, a little further back," Jillian answered. "And, believe it or not, it's one of my sillier attempts to appeal to the younger generation. It's all about horror."

I blinked a few times. My wife? She likes horror movies about as much as I did, which is to say, she *didn't*.

"Really?" I asked, as I leaned forward to see for myself what my wife had created. Unfortunately, even on the big-screen television it was too small to see much. "Cookbook Nook is a cookbook store, and a kitchen gadget store.

What type of display could you possibly have done?"

Jillian giggled. "Please. I have cake decorating books, fondant, ice picks, and a selection of themed candy, including those candy coffins, wax fangs, and gummy worms."

I nodded. "Right. Well, my guess is that one of those two displays is pertinent in some fashion."

"It can't possibly be the Sweden one," Harry decided. "It must have something to do with horror, bro."

The seven of us sat in collective silence as we stared at each other. Sweden or horror? How could it pertain to a bird being able to pick up radio transmissions?

"Right. We'll come back to these ones. Next up? Looks like we're still in Cookbook Nook."

"What are they looking at now?" Jillian asked. "I don't think my store has ever featured that much in one of your investigations."

"At the time, we didn't think we were investigating anything," I pointed out.

"True. All right, let's see." I rose from my chair and approached the television, which had Vance snickering. "Bite me, amigo. Now, I don't see anything out of the ordinary. Looks like I've aimed the camera at another part of Cookbook Nook, only in the other direction. More people were milling about, including …"

"Zachary!" Jillian exclaimed. "The mailman!"

"Yeah, I just noticed him," I admitted. "What about him?"

"Go back to the first picture."

A few finger swipes and we had backtracked to the first of the corgi clues. My eyes widened with disbelief.

"A postal truck," I whispered. "Everyone see it? It's

there, in the distance. It's quite unmistakable."

"Is it in all three of those pictures?" Vance asked.

I did a quick check. "Hmm, not quite. I see it here, in the first picture. In the second? It's still there, but farther away. And the third? I think it must have turned, 'cause I don't see it anymore."

"Neither do I," Dottie added.

I grabbed my soda and took a drink. "It's really not too surprising. I was snapping pictures as fast as I could. Plus, I couldn't see what I was aiming at. I was bound to get an extra shot in there."

Wrong again. When will I learn the dogs really *did* know more than us? I clearly needed to pay better attention. No, there are no extra pictures, but then again, none of us will figure that out until much later.

"And they fixated on the mailman in Jillian's store," Julie said, using a quiet voice. "All right, I'll ask. Why?"

I held up my hands. "I'm hoping that becomes evident the further we go."

Jillian produced a notebook and a pencil. Flipping it open, she started taking notes.

"First link appears to be the Post Office, got it. What's next?"

I moved to the next picture. What I saw had me shaking my head in bewilderment: it was the young detainee from Roseburg. The poor girl had been sitting at one of the many desks in that room, and looking at the picture, I could see she was wearing a forlorn expression on her face.

"Who is this?" Harry wanted to know.

"This was taken in Roseburg," I answered. "We were at the local police station, even though we weren't supposed to be, and …"

"What do you mean, you weren't supposed to be?" Julie interrupted.

"The Roseburg police chief is jealous of Sherlock and Watson's fame and reputation," Vance answered. "He didn't want anything to do with them, so when we asked whether or not we could come up there and check out their files on that bank heist ..."

"Hey, I remember reading about that!" Harry interrupted.

"... the chief was less than thrilled," I continued, ignoring the interruption. "So, Vance and I elected to stay away."

"Doesn't look that way to me, bro," Harry pointed out.

"A group of Sherlock and Watson admirers pulled us inside," Vance explained. "We didn't want to go, but they assured us the captain was away for lunch. We snuck in, we talked to the officer that we needed to, and snuck back out. Literally."

"And the girl?" Dottie asked. "What did she do?"

"Haven't a clue," I answered. "There were a bunch of desks, set about in this big square. Three were occupied, and only this one had a second person there. That's the one the dogs stopped at. I had to wait for the girl to look away before I took the picture."

"Zoom in on the picture," Jillian instructed. "Let's see if we can tell what the dogs were looking at."

The picture centered on the teenager and zoomed in until she was larger than life-sized.

"Looks like she's been through hell," Tori observed.

"Definitely," Julie agreed. "What is she holding?"

"Looks like a purse," Jillian decided. "That isn't too surprising. What else can we find? Well, she has a fair amount of jewelry on her: rings, earrings, and bracelets. I'm not sure if that's relevant or not."

Julie, sitting on Jillian's right, slid the notebook over and took the pencil when my wife held it up.

"Young girl with money," Julie said, as she scribbled notes. "Appears real. Clutching purse and … and … a book, I think. Zack, zoom out, would you? Okay, I count eight desks and you're right: three are occupied. I don't know if it helps, but I added it. Here you go, Jillian."

The notebook was returned.

"Thanks. Zachary, I don't think we're going to learn anything else. What's next?"

"Hey, that's *my* store!" Dottie exclaimed. "I forgot you took several pictures while you were in there."

"What are we looking at?" Vance wanted to know.

"I know that rack," Tori exclaimed. "It's the big one, just as you come in the door, on the right. Am I right, Dottie?"

"It's the new releases," Dottie said, as she nodded. "They sell the most, so I gave it the most space."

Jillian was nodding. "Smart. Play to your strengths. Okay, what can we tell about the picture?"

"Looks like just a bunch of books," I decided.

"I see *Heart of Éire*," Tori exclaimed, smiling. "Good for you, Dottie!"

The new bookstore owner smiled demurely. "Thanks. Zack's books sell amazingly well. In fact, I'm getting a little low on the Ireland book."

"I'll make sure to send you another shipment," I promised.

"Signed?" Dottie asked.

I glanced over at the Samuelsons. "Of course. All three

of us would love to."

Dottie beamed her appreciation. "Awesome! Thanks, Zack! You, too, Tori and Vance."

My detective friend, along with his wife, nodded. Once again, I flashed back to a time when Vance used to make fun of my profession. Knowing he was now a staunch supporter of my writing made me smile.

"Can anyone recognize anything else?" Jillian asked. "Zachary, what else do you have?"

I flipped to the next picture. "I can tell you this is the last one, guys. Jillian, do you recognize it?"

My wife smiled. "Well, I should. It's just around the corner. It's your kitchen. Is that when Sherlock was staring at the oven?"

I nodded. "That's the one."

"Why's Sherlock staring at the oven?" Harry wanted to know. "Was it time for dinner?"

I shook my head. "No, he was … well, yeah, if you want to look at it like that. Jillian was cooking a ham for dinner that night. Sherlock wouldn't leave the kitchen until I took a picture. Then, later, when we all came downstairs, the dogs went back to the kitchen. Sherlock resumed his staring, and Watson positioned herself so she could stare over here, in the living room."

"Why?" Vance asked. "Oh! Oh, I totally get it. Wow. That's impressive."

Several others in the room were wearing blank faces.

"For those of you who are lost," I said, pointing to the kitchen, "ham is in there, and radio is in here. Ham radio. That's how we knew what the source of these messages were."

Right about then, several conversations happened. Julie

was recalling how her father used to listen to his police scanner all the time. Vance mentioned one of his uncles used to have one of the ham radio setups. As for me and Jillian, well, we had slipped into yet another conversation about our new home. Then ... *this* happened.

"Woof."

Caught up in our own stories, laughing at jokes, and for the most part, enjoying ourselves, no one heard the telltale warning signs. And, if you know my dogs, it didn't go over well.

"WOOF."

We still didn't hear Sherlock's request for attention.

"AWWWOOOOOWOOWOOOOWOOO!"

Conversation came to an abrupt halt. Everyone turned to look at Sherlock, who was at the base of the stairs. Then, we all heard him give an exasperated snort and head back to the second floor.

"Was he telling us to be quiet?" I chuckled. Pushing back from the table, I rose to my feet. "I'll go see what he wants."

My wife placed her hand on mine. "Allow me."

"Thanks, dear."

After Jillian had departed, Vance cleared his throat.

"Tell me something, pal. This whole idea to tear this place down? Is that something you both want or just you? Or, for that matter, just Jillian?"

"Both. We had been wondering what to do about the living arrangements for a while now. I know she loves her house, and why wouldn't she? She's got Carnation Cottage looking picture-postcard-perfect, which is a technical term, by the way. As for me, well, I've got the room here, and the privacy. Lentari Cellars is sitting pretty, on fifty acres of land. My nearest neighbor is a quarter mile away. So, since we're not able to physically move Carnation Cottage here, it was decided to start fresh. This house was Aunt Bonnie's, including practically everything in here, so, it was an easy decision to just tear everything down."

Harry leaned forward. "Gonna do anything special with the place?"

I grinned at my friend. "Oh, you had better believe it. This place is gonna have more secrets than Highland House."

Vance raised his beer. "Now you're talking. If I ever had the ability to do the same thing ..."

"You're getting closer," I reminded my friend, which earned me smiles from both husband and wife.

"... I think I would ..."

"Zachary?" Jillian called.

There was something about the urgency in her voice which had me leaping to my feet. Everyone around the table did the same.

"Jillian? Are you okay?"

"Yes, but you need to see this. Hurry!"

"What is it?" I asked, as I hurried to the stairs.

"The ham radio? I know how Ruby has been getting his messages. I just heard a fourth message, and it was stuttering!"

EIGHT

The entire gang was crowded around the doorway into the pet room, and all of us were doing the same thing: trying to figure out how to get inside. Sherlock had returned to his spot on the couch where Watson and Ruby were seemingly waiting for us. The television was on, but it was back at the home screen again. The streaming service we used was good, but clearly not reliable, seeing how something kept locking up and forcing the app to kick us out. I reached for the remote to start it up again when Jillian swatted my hand aside.

"No, Zachary. Leave the TV here."

"Here? But there's nothing playing!"

Jillian smiled. "I think you'll find that something *is* playing."

"Who's playing the messages?" Harry's voice asked, from somewhere behind me. "Who's responsible for this?"

Jillian took my hand and lifted it up. "Why, Zack is."

I couldn't help it. My head tilted, just like a dog's.

"Wanna run that by me again? How did I become the one responsible for playing these messages for Ruby?"

Jillian pointed at the screen. "See for yourself. Your streaming service? It allows you to install all kinds of channels."

Nodding, I shrugged. "There's nothing new about that."

"Recognize all the channels you put in there?" Jillian challenged.

I focused on the screen. Admittedly, there *were* more channels than I remember seeing.

"Well, I don't remember that one, or that one, or … or … wow, there are a bunch of these I don't remember seeing. How'd they get on here?"

"Suggestions," Tori said, nodding. "We've got this same service at our house. There's an option, in the settings, where you can specify if you'd like to allow *suggestions* to be downloaded. Do you see the name of this one?"

Tori pointed at one of the unfamiliar squares, which denoted installed channels. It simply said Ham Radio.

"Well, shut my mouth and slap me silly," I muttered. "Wait. I can understand how it showed up, and why. What I don't understand, however, is how it's picking up transmissions in this area. I mean, how would it know where it's located?"

Vance pushed his way into the room. "I can answer that one, seeing how I actually know a little about the streaming stick you're using in here. It's in the same spot, in settings.

There's a place to enter your zip code, and if you do, then area-specific listings can be found."

"The zip code," I moaned. "I forgot about that, too. Now, what about the fact that the channel isn't loaded? I haven't played it before, and I haven't ever found it running. So, how could it be playing transmissions?"

"I was wondering that, too," Jillian admitted, "until I saw that the focus was on that particular channel."

"The what?" Dottie asked.

"Focus," Jillian repeated. "If I pick up the remote, and start using the directional arrows to pick a different channel, then the different channels will be selected. Do you see the white box highlighting the choice I make?"

It was Dottie's turn to push her way through. "Okay, I see it now."

"I haven't selected it yet," Jillian explained, "but the hardware knows I'm focusing my attention on that particular channel. Look what happens with most of these channels if the selector box falls on it."

The boxes became animated as they were selected, giving us previews of their programming. The ham radio channel didn't have any video preview to give, but what it *did* do was give another type of preview: audio.

"Watch when I put the focus back on the ham radio channel. Now, everyone be quiet, and let's see if we can hear it again."

"The wh-wheel is c-c-come full c-circle: I am h-h-here."

"Well, would you look at that," Vance commented. "I wouldn't have thought …"

"The wh-wheel is c-c-come full c-circle: I am h-h-here! I am h-h-here!"

We all turned to look at Ruby, who was now bobbing

up and down on the perch I had installed in the room for her. I smiled at the bird and tapped my shoulder. Moments later, Ruby was nuzzled against my neck.

"That's a good girl, Ruby. And Sherlock? Watson? You guys did it, pal. You let us know something was happening. Good job! You both get treats tonight."

Both corgi nubs were wiggling so much that their entire bodies were wriggling. Sherlock rushed to my side first, intent on receiving the most praise. Watson reared up on her hind legs and waited for me to pick her up.

"And you didn't want to adopt any dogs," Harry scoffed. "They've worked wonders on you."

"You make it sound like I was a basket case until they became a part of my life."

Harry held up his hands. "Well, bro? Isn't that the case?"

"Yeah, maybe. Shut up."

Laughter bounced around the room. Setting Watson back on the couch, I turned to Vance and pointed at the screen.

"Okay, if *that* is the source of the transmissions, then what now? Can we track one of those messages to its source?"

My detective friend shrugged. "I really don't know, pal."

Tori held up a hand. "I might be able to help here. I remember one of my students mentioning his father is a member of the PV ham radio club. They could probably give you a hand."

"Would you pass my number along to them?" I asked. "Have them give me a call at their earliest convenience."

The only thing I can say is that the earliest convenience

for that particular family was the exact moment they got the message. I know this, because the following day, not long after school would have started, I got a phone call. It was the student's father, inviting me to visit his house so he could show off his amateur radio setup.

The guy the dogs and I were going out to meet went by the name of Pete Westecott. Tori tells me that Mr. Westecott had proclaimed himself leader of the club, insisting he was more heavily invested in the hobby than anyone else. Pulling up to his house, I could see why.

The street I was on was a nice, quiet side street located about ten minutes from downtown PV. All the houses were of average size, all were maintained, and their lawns were nice and clean. Pete's house had all of the above *and* had the most complex, tallest antenna I've ever seen hooked up to a residential house. I later learned these are the more popular high-gain antennas used to monitor the HF, VHF, and UHF bands.

"Like it?" a friendly voice asked, after I placed Sherlock and Watson on the ground and craned my neck to study the huge antenna.

The owner of the voice was slightly older than me, had the same build, and was probably just as tall. He wore a thick, handlebar mustache that had more gray than black in it, and a thin set of wire-rimmed eyeglasses. He seemed very approachable, which was a pleasant surprise. I think I was expecting a much smaller, bookish-type of fellow. He crushed my hand in a handshake.

"As with any antenna, the higher you can go, the farther you can reach. Pete Westecott. It's good to meet you, Mr. Anderson. My wife and I have been a fan of your winery for several years now."

"Thanks for that, Pete. Well, that thing's a monster. How far can you reach?"

"When the weather conditions are at their peak, I can easily reach half-way 'round the world. I think the farthest I've ever picked up a signal is from Madagascar."

"Wow. And here I was expecting you to say ... I don't know, maybe Idaho?"

Pete laughed and then caught sight of the dogs. "Oh, Bethany is going to be so jealous! We saw these two in England, with the Queen!"

I raised a hand. "You know, rumor has it I was there, too."

A look of horror appeared on Pete's face. "Oh, I'm so sorry. That's not what I meant. I know you were there, too, Mr. Anderson."

"Don't sweat it. And call me Zack."

Pete turned to gaze admiringly up at the antenna. "Thanks, Zack. So, you want to learn more about amateur radio? You came to the right place. This baby? It's called a Yagi. Since you probably don't know what that is ..."

"Which I don't."

"... I can tell you it's a directional antenna that radiates signals in one main direction."

"Only one direction?" I repeated, confused. "What if ..."

"I'm way ahead of you," Pete interrupted. He pointed at the base of the antenna, hidden from view on the back side of his house. "It's all computer controlled. If I want to point the antenna in another direction, then I tell my computer, and it gives the command to the base to rotate the entire thing. Come on, I'll show you my base of operations."

We stepped into Pete's house, and one glance around told me that it was tastefully furnished, clean, and comfortable. Pete led us down a short flight of stairs to the house's main floor, then to a hallway on the right. At the end of the hallway was a closed metal door.

"My man cave," Pete explained, as he produced a set of keys and unlocked the door.

"Your wife isn't allowed in?"

Pete snickered. "Oh, sure, she is. Only, she wants nothing to do with what's on the other side of that door."

Holding the door open, the dogs and I stepped through and into what I can only describe as another world. Everywhere I looked, blinking lights winked back at me. Strange components with tiny dials sat on shelves the way you or I would display books. Many were humming, some were even emitting a soft static-type noise. Several headsets hung on pegs, an array of microphones were on the opposite wall, and an assortment of small two-way radios sat in their chargers on yet another.

"You have quite a collection here, Pete," I said, as I looked around. "I can't even imagine what most of these are responsible for doing."

"Each has its own task," Pete assured me. "Plus, I've got replacements for each area, and once a month I'll fire everything up for a week, just to make sure all is in tip-top condition. I have another three days before I'll power off probably two-thirds of what you see here."

"Impressive. Expensive?"

Pete laughed out loud. "Oh, I'll say. How does one marriage sound to you?"

Sobering, I stared at my new friend and wondered how I was supposed to react.

"Oh, don't worry," Pete said, correctly interpreting my hesitation. "My first wife wasn't the one for me. She thought all of this was just a passing fancy and I shouldn't devote so much time to it."

"Everyone has their passion," I returned. "For you, it's this."

"And you?" Pete asked.

"Writing."

"That's right. I heard you're a writer. I'll have to ask my wife if she's read anything by you. Now, you're out here, and you're in my secret hideout, so to speak. What can I do for you?"

"Can ham radio transmissions be traced?"

"As in, figure out where the person was when he—or she—sent their transmission?"

I nodded. "Yes. That's exactly what I'm here to find out."

Pete pulled his chair away from the main command center, spun it around, and sat down. He indicated a smaller chair nearby that I should take. Only when we were settled, and both dogs were stretched out by my feet, did Pete continue.

"You'll be pleased to know that, yes, it *is* possible to trace a ham radio transmission."

I gave a celebratory fist pump. "Awesome. That's exactly what I wanted to hear."

"Don't celebrate yet," Pete warned. "Yes, it's possible, but no, it's highly unlikely anyone would ever take the time to trace a signal."

My elation evaporated and I'm sure the look on my face spoke volumes.

"Let me explain," Pete continued. "In order to track

a signal made by ham radio equipment, you have to use triangulation. I assume you know what that means?"

I nodded. "Sure, I'm just not sure how that pertains to this."

"I'll tell you how. Let's say you're an emergency responder and you're trying to trace the signal of someone who needs help, but woe of woes, you've got nothing but acres and acres of open country in front of you. What do you do? Well, we would need to have at least three multiple directional finding stations in order to figure out where it came from. Think of them as mobile radio stations."

"Okay."

"With me so far?"

"Yeah, I think so."

"To find the source of a signal, you must be in range."

I nodded. "Naturally."

"The searchers would have to move in the direction the signal is strongest."

"Makes sense."

"And finally, the point where all three mobile stations intersect would be the location of the ham radio."

"Hmm. I think I see where you're going with this."

Pete nodded. "Right? It might appear simple at first, but to do a search like this is incredibly time consuming. No one is going to take the time to triangulate the radio. Why? Because what we radio enthusiasts like to chat about is incredibly insignificant. Plus, it's not easy to find someone with access to three mobile stations. Oh, I should also mention that the person triangulating the signal would need to know the time and date of the transmission."

"Which we don't know," I admitted. "It'd be a best guess at most."

"I haven't even gotten to the hard part yet," Pete said, giving me an apologetic smile. He reached down to pat each of the corgis. "Weather plays an important part when doing a search like that. Clouds, rain, and even the wind can cause dispersal of the signal."

"The wind?" I asked, trying hard to keep the skepticism from my voice.

"Oh, sure. If the winds blow strong enough, then the trees start shaking, and just like that, your line of sight gets blocked, which means no signal."

"Ah. I get it."

"Sorry, Zack. I know that isn't what you want to hear. The answer to your question, can the signals be tracked? Technically speaking, yes, but I doubt very much you could around here. This is Oregon. Look outside. When was the last time you saw the sun?"

Laughing, I bid our new friend farewell. On our way back to town, I started thinking about what the next step was going to be. Now that we know *how* Ruby is hearing those transmissions, I have that ham radio channel playing on every television in the house. Plus, Vance and Tori are doing the same at their place. If the guy making those Shakespearean references says anything else, we're going to know about it the instant it happens.

We were on Main Street, approaching Cookbook Nook, when I had one of those episodes you've probably seen on the cartoons. It's the one where the nervous cat keeps getting spooked by that yappy little puppy, and the cat ends up hanging upside down from the ceiling. Well, that's what happened to me in my Jeep. I had just started scanning the area, looking for a parking space, when Sherlock and Watson must've thought we passed Satan himself. The fur on both corgis' backs stood straight up and both started barking as though their lives depended on it. Honestly? I'm surprised I didn't drive right into the side of the nearest building, which would have been Jillian's, so I dodged *two* bullets there.

"Holy smokes, guys. What are you trying to do, give me a heart attack? Stop barking, would you? Sherlock, take it down a notch. There's nothing out there that …"

Noticing he was being ignored, Sherlock switched to something a little more likely to get attention.

"Awwwwooooooo! Awwwooooowooooowoooo!"

"Ooooo!" Watson agreed.

Didn't we already move past the corgi clue bit? They wanted to me to take another picture? What was out there, anyway?

I saw a parking spot not too far from Cookbook Nook's front entrance. Quickly pulling in, I threw the parking brake on and looked around. There wasn't much, I'm afraid. I saw a couple of pedestrians on either side of the street. There was what looked like a family of tourists getting ready to slip inside one of the restaurants. And traffic? On Main Street, the speed limit was set at a breathtaking, sound wave shattering *twenty*. The cars we passed were still visible, which were a couple of sedans, one box truck making deliveries, and a squat vehicle that looked as though it had the steering wheel on the wrong side of the car. A few moments later, it came to me. The Post Office has been known to sell off their older vehicles. It was a converted mail Jeep.

The color drained from my face. A converted US Mail Jeep? And the dogs went ballistic? Weren't there a couple of corgi clues that featured a postal vehicle of some sort?

And I'm pretty sure I took a picture of a mailman in Cookbook Nook. All I had to do now is verify that this retired mail car was what was driving my dogs nuts.

"Hang on, guys. If we pull out right now, we'll be able to see if this Jeep thingamajig is what you want me to look at. Here we go."

Without giving too much thought about what this must look like, I executed a swift U-turn, just in time to see Jillian come out the front door and give me a questioning look. I held up my phone as I passed her and waggled it. Then, I watched her hurry back inside her store.

Accelerating as much as I could without attracting attention, and weaving close to the oncoming traffic, I watched the dogs as we passed.

"Awwwwwooooooo!" Sherlock howled. He only had eyes for the Jeep.

Watson whined and, together, they stood up on the back seat of my own Jeep to look out the rear window. Well, you couldn't get any more certain than that. Right then, my cell rang. Of course, it was Jillian.

"Zachary? Is everything okay?"

"I think I'm following the guy who made the transmissions."

"What? Are you serious? How do you know?"

"Sherlock and Watson, that's how. They didn't just woof at me, my dear. They howled so loud, and for so long, that I think I need a new set of underwear."

I heard a slight giggle on the phone.

"And," I continued, "this vehicle is, er, *was* used as a postal service Jeep. And, get this. Now that I'm getting closer to it, I can confirm it has two super-long antennas coming off the back bumper, which means it has some type of fancy radio inside."

"I'm calling Vance."

"Do that, would you? And have him call me. I'm going to follow this guy and see where he goes."

Not ten seconds later, Vance's name appeared on my phone.

"Hello?"

"Zack? What's going on? Jillian called and said …"

"I think I'm following the guy from the Roseburg bank heist," I said, as soon as I heard my friend take a breath.

"What?! How did you …? Where did you …? Are you sure?"

"The dogs. They spooked me so bad that they almost made me get into an accident. Plus, the vehicle he's driving is a former US Mail Jeep."

"A former … I'll be damned."

"It gets better. This Jeep has several huge antennas on it."

"Where are you? I'm sending some units your way."

"Uh, oh. I think the jig is up. He's driving erratically, and starting to swerve."

"How close are you following him?" Vance angrily asked. "Hold on." A few moments of silence passed. "I'm going for my car. I'll be there shortly!"

"Vance?"

"Yeah?"

"Did you give the order to have backup sent my way?"

"I just did, yeah. I muted the phone. Why?"

"This Jeep just took off! This has to confirm he's our guy, right? A scanner! Vance, what do you want to bet he has a police scanner in his vehicle? No wonder he's fleeing. He must have heard us! Or, more specifically, he heard you!"

"Damn. Zack, if this is the right guy, then he's extremely

dangerous. Don't get anywhere near him."

"Oh, don't you worry about that. I'm about fifty feet back from him right now."

"Where are you?"

"Highway 238, heading northeast, out of town. I think … I think he's angling for the Siskiyou National Forest. Vance, if he gets in there, it's gonna be almost impossible to find him."

I heard the wail of a police siren from behind me.

"Just heard from the captain," Vance said, after a few moments of silence had passed. "Zack, you are hereby ordered to cease and desist. Do not pursue this guy. They have already killed one person. Don't give him any reason to do it again."

"If I don't follow him, then he'll get away!" I protested.

"Then he gets away," Vance said. "Stop pursuing. Do it, buddy."

I took my foot off the gas and allowed my Jeep to come to a stop. A police cruiser raced past me. Once it did, I turned my vehicle around and headed back into town.

"Fine. I've stopped and am heading back."

"Good. Now, kindly stay out of the way and let the professionals do their job. I'm betting they'll have our guy before sunset."

"You're that sure?"

"Seeing how we've got two choppers from Medford and one from Grants Pass on the way, I'll say, yes, I'm sure. We're also assembling a ground team, and I just received word Roseburg is sending their own group of guys down. We'll have him before the end of the night."

One hour. It took only one hour. Someone should've told the guy that, if you're actively being pursued, and you've got your own off-the-grid house where you've been hiding, you really ought to put out your fire. The ground assault crew came, they saw, and the rest is history.

"They got him, buddy!" Vance shouted, nearly two hours later. "One Jake Plinski is now in custody."

"Is he the short dude who killed the security guard or is he the taller guy?"

"He's shorter than me, but not by much," Vance reported.

"You caught the taller guy, got it. What happened to the short dude, the killer?"

"Mr. Plinski wouldn't say. The two robbers evidently split up. The only thing we could determine is that our friend, the Jeep driver, has spent the last couple of days driving around town."

"What? What for? Was he trying to get caught?"

"He *was* caught, buddy."

"No, I mean … you'd think if you were an accessory to a major bank robbery, where a person was brutally murdered, then you wouldn't want to be out wandering around a town. In public."

At this time, I was back in my house and was just sitting down to wait for Jillian to return home when Vance called with his news. As for now? I was met with silence.

"Did I lose you?" I asked.

"I'm still here," Vance reported. "I see your point, Zack. What do you think Plinski was doing in town?"

A notion dawned on me, and it had me smiling. "Corgi clues."

"What? Did you say corgi clues?"

"I did. Listen, I think our man Plinski was doing the same thing we were doing: trying to figure out the clues.

He received transmission from his accomplice and was trying to figure out what they meant."

"The transmissions," Vance whispered. "He couldn't decipher their meaning, could he?"

"That'd be my guess."

"This is both good and bad," Vance decided. "I just wish we could figure them out before he does."

"We tried," I complained. "Nobody around here knows enough about Shakespeare to …"

"What is it?" my friend asked, after I trailed off.

"No," I moaned.

"Huh?"

"Oh, crap on a cracker. It couldn't be that easy, could it?"

"What? If you've thought of something, Zack, now's the time to spill it. What do you have?"

"What is southern Oregon known for?"

"Say what?"

"Southern Oregon. What's it known for?"

I could actually *hear* Vance rolling his eyes.

"I don't know. Blueberries? Wine? Apples?"

"Come on, pal," I urged. "Think harder."

"If you've got something, Zack, just tell me, okay?"

"Vance, the transmissions are all about Shakespeare. We already know we're not that proficient about him, so if we wanted to learn more about him, or maybe catch a play or two, where would we go?"

"I don't know. YouTube?"

"I'll give you a hint: it's located in southwestern Oregon and attracts hundreds of thousands of visitors a year." When my friend fell silent, I had no choice to blurt it out. "How about a Shakespeare festival?"

The line fell silent.

"Vance? Are you still there?"

More silence.

"When is it?" Vance finally asked.

"From February to October."

"And you're just now thinking about this?" Vance demanded.

"Hey, you've lived here longer than I have," I answered, growing defensive. "I could ask you the same thing!"

"Do you really think the answer is there?" Vance wanted to know.

"We have four messages, and they all focus on Shakespeare. One of the two guys was caught here, in Pomme Valley. Ashland is only about twenty minutes away. What do *you* think?"

"I think the cash is stashed in Ashland," Vance decided, growing excited. "You up for a road trip?"

I grabbed the leashes and called for the dogs. "Who's driving, you or me?"

NINE

The town of Ashland, Oregon, spread out before us. With a population of nearly 22,000 residents, it easily dwarfed PV. Factor in the amount of visitors it gets from February through October, the months the Oregon Shakespearean Festival, or OSF for short, is active, then it can easily add hundreds of thousands of visitors each year.

"Be honest. How many times have you come down here? I figure it's probably at least four times."

I looked at Vance and grinned. "I'll tell if you will. Tori is a history teacher. If she's a fan of Shakespeare, then you've probably been here more than I have."

"She says she enjoys reading Shakespeare," Vance began, "but I'm pretty sure that was only during the college years."

"Have you?" I challenged.

"What?"

"Ever read any of Shakespeare's stuff? Plays, tragedies, or even a sonnet or two?"

"Only with the threat of failing a class," Vance said, giving me a grin. "How people lived their lives in the past holds no interest for me."

"Odd thing to say, seeing how Tori is such a history buff."

"Right? You know what they say: opposites attract. Well, let's have it. How many times have you been here?"

I held up a hand with two fingers displayed.

"Twice? Only two times? Come on. You're kidding."

"I'm not," I confirmed. "Neither of us is too big on Shakespeare. Oh, don't get me wrong, I've read some of his work, but like you, it was for school. High school, in fact. I didn't have to take any Elizabethan poetry classes in college."

The OSF, started in the mid-1930s, has grown each year in popularity until it became, quite frankly, the largest regional repertory theater in the United States. In case you're wondering, a repertory theater is a U.K. theater in which a resident company presents works from a specified repertoire. Sound like an official definition? Well, it should be. As soon as I saw the term, I checked Wikipedia to see what it was.

"I can understand," Vance suddenly began, "the desire to come visit this place and watch your favorite shows, but ..."

"Plays," I interrupted.

"Fine, whatever. You come here to watch your favorite Shakespeare plays, so ..."

"Shakespearean," I corrected. "His name is Shakespeare, but if you talk about one of his works, the adjective form of his name is Shakespearean."

"Correct me again and you're walking home," Vance grumbled.

"Sorry. I'll shut up now."

My friend gripped the steering wheel that much tighter. "Good. Now, where was I?"

"You mentioned something about coming here to watch your favorite play. After that? I don't know."

"Okay, thanks. As I was saying, before being interrupted—twice—is that, sure, you enjoy this type of thing, and you come here to watch the shows. Plays. Whatever."

"Is there a question in there somewhere?" I asked.

We both heard a collar shake from behind us. Turning in my seat, I saw that both corgis were awake, and were watching the passing scenery. Good. Hopefully, they'll zero in on something.

"Anything?" Vance asked.

"Nope. I think Sherlock was stretching."

"All right. My question: if you, a fan, come here to watch something you're interested in, do you really have to come dressed as *that*?"

Vance pointed, and I looked. In fact, the dogs and I all looked. There, walking along the side of the street, was a group of teenagers, and all were attired in period pieces. Long, wavy dresses for the girls, and for the boys, jerkins, breeches, and stockings pulled up to their knees.

"Maybe they're performers?" I suggested.

"Then, what about them?" Vance asked, as he pointed to a different group.

This time, there was a group of nearly twenty people, of varying age. I saw kids as young as ten with adults that were easily older than me. All of them were wearing the same themed attire.

"It's no different than dressing up for a Star Trek convention," I decided.

"Have you?" Vance asked, as a smile formed on his face.

"What, dress up for a Comic-Con? No. I like going to them, and I like the chance of meeting the actors, or maybe getting an autograph from them, but dressing up? I don't think I even liked it as a kid for Halloween. Besides, if I was going to do it, I'd choose Star Wars over Star Trek on any day of the week."

Vance directed his Oldsmobile sedan over to a parking lot and parked near the bus drop-off area off of Pioneer Street.

"I'm really not a fan of this place," my detective friend admitted. "Any time I hear someone quote Shakespeare, or else try to read something on my own, it feels like I'm trying to learn another language. Hey, I have a question. Are all of these buildings part of the festival?"

I pointed at the huge domed structure ahead of us, on the right.

"See that one? It's the Allen Elizabethan Theater. It may look like it's an indoor auditorium, but it's actually an outdoor theater."

"Come rain or shine," Vance muttered.

"It's the closest approximation to what a period English theater would look like," I explained. "Then again, there's another over there. See that one? With what looks like a huge half dome behind it?"

"Yeah, I do. What's the deal with those, anyway? Why make the stages look so … weird?"

"Acoustics," I answered. I may not know much about Shakespeare, or his work, but I did know a thing or two about the time frame, having written a few period pieces based in sixteenth-century London. "Remember, there are no microphones or speakers. The performer on the stage has to be heard in all the seats. Those theaters are very delicately balanced, so you'll be able to hear everything that's spoken."

"Hmm," Vance grunted. I guess it was his way of saying he approved of the explanation. "Where are we headed? Have the dogs noticed anything yet?"

I glanced down at Sherlock and Watson. Having always enjoyed their many admirers, the corgis were trying to look in all directions at the same time. To be fair, I usually didn't take them to huge crowds like this. At least, not when we were pursuing someone.

"They're people watching," I reported.

Vance was silent for a moment before nodding. "Good. Maybe they'll spot something we don't. So, where do we go?"

"I say we check out the three theaters. You see the big one over there, and the smaller one there. The third is down that street and to the left, just on the other side of Carpenter Hall."

"Carpenter Hall? Okay, Mr. English Professor, how do you know all these things? You said you were only here a few times."

I started pointing out various landmarks.

"That's Carpenter Hall, and on the other side of it, to the southeast, is Thomas Theater. Administration offices are on our right, there's a gift shop also on the right, and this here? This is called the Green Show Stage. It's where plays are performed that don't charge for tickets."

"Spill, pal. How do you know so much?"

I held up a tri-folded pamphlet. "I picked this up right after we left the parking lot. It's a tourist map, showing where everything is. Why? Did I sound like I knew what I was doing?"

"Yeah, you did," Vance admitted. "That's how I knew something was up."

My mouth closed with an audible snap. "Well played, amigo. Spoken like a true smarty-pants."

"How often do the shows run?" Vance inquired.

I consulted my map. "Let's see. Looks like at any given time, there are five to eleven plays offered, in a daily rotation, and that happens six days a week in the three different theaters."

Vance was nodding. "Something is always playing. That's cool, I guess."

I pointed at the distant domed structure. "There are usually three plays held there, in the big outdoor one. Just over there, is the Angus Bowmer Theater. Hmm, it says here that this particular theater is the most traditional of the three, and has an average of four or five plays a day. And, for the record, it's all indoors."

"I thought you said the big outdoor one was the most representative of what an English theater would look like?"

My eyes widened as I realized my gaffe. "That's just great. Methinks I needeth to talk with mine publisher, 'cause methinks I got yonder facts majorly wrongeth."

Vance gave me a look, which said I was officially off my rocker. "Dork. Don't talk like that. You don't want me to lump you with these people, do you?"

"Hey, they're just passionate about Shakespeare," I said, as a group of giggling school children, on a presumed field trip, hurried around us. Several of the kids patted the dogs on the head as they passed. I had to wrap the leash around my hand a few times in case Sherlock and Watson switched to their Clydesdale personas and yanked my sorry butt after them. "No, you don't. We're here to work, not play."

Sherlock snorted once, turned to look back at me, and then shook himself off.

Vance turned to the Green Show Stage and hooked a thumb at it. "What's with this one? Why don't they charge for tickets there?"

"The only thing I can find is that it must be where the non-Shakespeare plays are performed."

"This is the OSF," Vance pointed out. "Why play something here that isn't Shakespeare?"

"Why not?" I countered. "If the play was written in the same time frame, why limit the productions to just one playwright? Shakespeare isn't the only person who wrote plays in the sixteenth century, you know."

Vance shrugged and looked pointedly down at the dogs. When neither corgi showed any inclination to take the lead, Vance sighed and headed toward the closest theater, which was the Angus Bowmer. Thankfully, there wasn't anything happening there at this exact moment. But, from the look of the frenetic activity on the stage, a production must be getting close to starting.

"Showtime is in twenty minutes," a security guard announced, as he stepped into our path. "If you'd like to come back then, you'll be able to …"

The guard trailed off as Vance pulled his badge and held it out for the guard to inspect.

"I'm terribly sorry, officer."

"It's Detective Vance Samuelson, of the Pomme Valley police department," Vance corrected. "My associates and I would just like to look around a little, if you don't mind."

The guard stepped out of the way. "Not at all. Help yourself. The next show is scheduled to begin in about twenty minutes."

"Which one?" I asked.

"Othello. Seen it before?" the guard politely inquired.

"Read it in high school," I reported. "Don't ask me what it was about. Those memories were purged eons ago."

The guard laughed. "No worries. If you'll … corgis? You're using corgis to help you on a case? Wait. Wait! Pomme Valley? Police corgis? Could these two be …"

The guard trailed off as I held a finger to my lips.

"This is Sherlock and Watson," I confirmed. "Please don't say anything out loud. Let's face it. These two dogs are more popular than any of us, and we don't want to attract a crowd, all right?"

The guard nodded. "You got it, sir. See the hall behind me? Follow it until you get to a set of double doors. They should be open. Go through, and then keep to the left. It'll open into the theater. There'll be a lot of activity in there, so please try not to get in the way."

"We won't," Vance promised.

Once inside the theater, we could see that the type of seating for the audience resembled a stadium, only the levels were much steeper than anything I've ever seen before. The two times I've watched plays here, at the OSF, were at the much larger Allen Elizabethan Theater. This theater's seating was wrapped around an inner stage, and according to the pamphlet I was holding, none of the seats were more than fifty-five feet from the stage.

As the guard had informed us, there were all kinds of people bustling about on stage. Scaffolding was set up, with several painters applying touchup to what looked like the sides of a castle wall. The first two rows of seats also had some type of protective film on them. I guess they wanted to make certain no paint splatter could damage the seats. A show was set to start here in less than half an hour? There's no way.

The more I watched, as we followed the dogs blindly around the theater, the more I knew I was going to be wrong. The speed and efficiency of this crew would put any NASCAR pit crew to shame. The instant painting was done, the friggin' castle wall was sucked up, into the rafters, and a different wall was lowered. In fact, it was dropped to the ground so fast that I thought for sure it was going to make contact with the floor, yet it didn't. A different painter hurriedly climbed into the scaffolding and put some finishing touches on the large prop.

"Anything?" Vance wanted to know.

"We've been from one side of the theater to the other," I reminded my friend. "I've kept a close eye on the dogs. Not one of them has given the slightest indication we're in the right place."

"Damn. All right, what do you think? Should we try another theater?"

"Sure. Let's walk them around that open Green Show Stage and see if they pick anything up."

They didn't. No matter how hard we tried, and seeing how the highest number of plays were held in this free venue, Sherlock and Watson acted like they couldn't give a fig about any of it.

"There are no seats out here," Vance observed. "Oh, I get it. The staff puts out temporary seating?"

I checked my pamphlet.

"From the pictures, it looks like this huge lawn right here serves as the seating area. Most people are shown to be sitting directly on the grass. But, I will say that I do see some people sitting in folding chairs. If I were to guess, then I'd say that those people probably brought their own chairs. Sherlock? Watson? Come on. Let's walk around."

As much fun as the two corgis had sniffing and frolicking along the grass, nothing attracted their attention there, either.

Vance pointed at the small cement pad at the bottom of the curved hill.

"Well, we're here. Let's go check the stage. Maybe something happened down there and Sherlock is just waiting to let us know."

He wasn't. Just as before, both corgis sniffed around a few times. Growing bored, they stretched out on the cool concrete and stared at us, as though *we* were inconveniencing *them*.

"I'm sorry, your Royal Canineships. Is this not fun for you guys? Want to go home? Come on. We need to keep looking."

Next up was the much larger Allen Elizabethan Theater. Holding nearly twelve hundred spectators at a time, this particular theater was originally built in 1935, but suffered through a fire in 1940, which destroyed most of the stage. After WWII, it was decided the theater, after undergoing several remodels to increase seating, was deemed a fire hazard and in 1958, it was torn down.

Needless to say, the residents of the area loved their theater, so after raising a quarter of a million dollars, the facility was rebuilt and had its reopening nearly a year later. Over the years, various improvements were built, more seats were added, and with ambient noise rising in the area, the curved half-dome was added so that the actors could continue to be heard. Add in a three million dollar grant from Microsoft co-founder Paul Allen, and the theater was renamed the Allen Elizabethan Theater.

Twelve hundred seats. Vance, the dogs, and I spent nearly an hour in the empty theater as we canvassed the stage, seating, orchestra platform, the dome, and so on. Not one freakin' woof from either corgi.

Not to be deterred, we moved to the smallest of the three theaters, the Thomas Theater. This indoor theater had three sections of seats: left, center, and right. Each section held ninety seats, which placed the total count to around two-hundred seventy. However, my pamphlet said it could go up to three-hundred sixty, but I wasn't going to argue the point.

This particular theater was in the midst of a production, The Tempest, according to the posters displayed on the walls in the lobby. Vance and I eyed each other and then looked down at the dogs. Sherlock and Watson's ears were straight up and swiveling left and right, like radar antennas. Thankfully, neither dog wanted to check anything out and, instead, pulled us back to the outside door.

"That could've been awkward," Vance chuckled. "For once in my life, I'm glad they didn't find anything in there."

"That makes two of us. Okay, that's all three theaters. Four, if we count the Green one."

"Where to now, Mr. PBS?"

"Mr. PBS?" I repeated, raising an eyebrow.

Vance pointed at the informational pamphlet I was still holding.

"Where does that thing say we should go now?"

"It doesn't say we need to go anywhere," I pointed out. "But, if I wanted to venture a guess, I'd say ... hey, Vance, check this out. See what it says here?"

"Where?"

"Right here. It ... you're not wearing your glasses."

"Bite me, pal."

"No, I'm serious. I'm not trying to tease. It says Hay-Patterson Rehearsal Center. It's next to these educational classrooms."

"Educational classrooms?" Vance repeated. "Let's go take a look."

A quick, ten-minute walk brought us to where we needed to be, but the moment we arrived, all four of us slammed on the brakes. I heard Vance groan. Both corgis, however, started wiggling with excitement. I guess I shouldn't be too surprised. After all, the pamphlet did say *educational classrooms*.

Nearly five hundred kids, assembled into eight different groups, collectively looked up at us as we rounded the corner. A cheer broke out and just like that, eight different teachers, and twice as many parent volunteers, all had their hands full. Shouts of how cute the dogs were echoed inside the large amphitheater. Most of them wanted us to approach their groups so they (the kids) could meet the dogs.

One of the teachers broke away from her group and approached us.

"You fellows seem lost," the woman cheerfully told us. "Can I help you find anything?"

Vance flipped open his badge.

"I'm terribly sorry to interrupt, ma'am. We're here on official business, just looking around. This festival might have a connection to a case we're working, and we're just checking to see if our dogs notice anything."

The woman's eyes dropped to the ground and she suddenly gasped. She looked at Vance, shook her head, and then over at me. That's when her eyes widened with surprise. I have a feeling the dogs and I were just recognized.

"You're Zachary Anderson! And that means these two are Sherlock and Watson! I saw you on television, accepting an award from the Queen of England! Oh my goodness! Sheryl! Sheryl, come here! I ... sorry. Er, Ms. Dodson? Come over here, quick!"

A second woman arrived. "I can't stay long. You've seen my kids. They'll chew you up and spit you out if someone isn't there to ..."

The newest arrival trailed off as she looked at the corgis. Then, her gaze lifted until she was looking at me. I watched those eyes widen to the size of saucers. She then slapped a hand over her mouth.

"That's right," the first teacher confirmed. "It's Sherlock and Watson! They're working a case!"

"Here?" the teacher asked, as she tried to regain her composure.

Thinking fast, I stepped forward.

"Look, ladies, you're right. These two are Sherlock and Watson. I hadn't realized they'd be getting as much attention, or recognition, as they have recently, but you're right. We're working a case. Would you care to help us?"

Both teachers wordlessly nodded.

"I hope you know what you're doing, buddy," I heard Vance murmur.

I grinned at the two teachers. "Bring your kids over here. I'm afraid we don't have time to meet them on an individual basis, but they can certainly see them up close. I think there might be a way for you guys to help us."

Both teachers turned on their heels, faced their group of kids who were—surprisingly—quiet as they were studying the hushed conversation their teachers were having. Once they saw their teachers beckon them over, they made a free-for-all dash across the amphitheater. Giving the adults a few minutes to get their excited charges under control, I cleared my throat and pointed at the dogs.

"Now, no screaming or yelling, as it'll probably spook the dogs, but with a show of hands, who among you has heard of two crime-fighting dogs by the name of Sherlock and Watson?"

Nearly three-quarters of the hands went up.

"That's them. This is Sherlock, and this is Watson. We're working a case. Would you like to help us? Again, hands only, please. Raise them up if yes, otherwise keep them down if no."

All were raised.

"Good. Here's what I need you to do. Look around here. People come to this festival either as you guys do, meaning in a group, or with a family, significant other, and so on. We're looking for anyone who *doesn't* fit that description, meaning someone on their own. We're looking for a short, small guy, er, adult male, who is more than likely by himself, and doing everything he can to not be noticed."

"Like a homeless guy?" one boy asked.

I looked at Vance, who shrugged.

"Sure, I guess. I can't imagine you'd find many homeless people hanging around the theaters."

"This isn't going to work," Vance told me, lowering his voice to almost a whisper. "You're talking about the first guy? The one still on the run?"

"Yes. What's wrong?"

"Zack, he would have been here several weeks ago. They obviously weren't here then."

"True," I said, shaking my head, "but think about it. Plinski couldn't follow the clues. What's that mean? The, um, well, what we're looking for is still out there. Remember, when those two came through here the first time, every cop in the state was probably on their tail. They didn't have much time to hide that which they stole." If you hadn't noticed, I was electing *not* to publicly announce we were looking for a load of cash. "I'm thinking that the two of them must've become separated at some point. Tiny Dude, as I'm calling him, is in serious hot water. He's wanted, and in a bad way. So, he knows he can't show his face. But, he also knows that there's a better than average chance their ill-gotten gains will be found. What does he do? He tries to signal his partner about where he stashed it."

Vance was nodding. "All right, I'm liking where this is going. Go on."

"Right. Now, think about what's happened. Plinski recently got himself captured. That means there's no one left for Tiny Dude to rely on to recover the goods. Therefore …?"

"Therefore," Vance continued, growing excited, "he decides to risk himself getting caught so he can get here first. Zack, you're a genius!"

"Man, I wish I had been recording that," I said, as I gave my friend a smile.

"Don't let it go to your head," Vance warned. "Do you really think he's here?"

I pointed at the dogs. "I don't know. I'd like to think that, if he was, these two would alert us to his presence."

My detective friend was silent as he considered. After a few moments, he started to nod.

"All right, I guess I can get on board with that." He looked back out at the crowd. "Kids? I'm Detective Vance Samuelson, of the Pomme Valley PD. I don't know how long you guys have been enjoying the festival, but my friend here is right. We're looking for a very bad man who took something that wasn't his. If you see him, or if you think you've seen him, then you need to let us know, all right?"

"I'm not putting my kids in danger," the second teacher, Ms. Dodson, stated, matter-of-factly.

"Good for you," Vance praised. "I never would, either. I'm simply asking that, in your earlier explorations of the area, if you, or any of your kids, noticed someone that made you look twice."

"I haven't, no."

"The homeless guy," the same young boy said, drawing nods from his fellow students.

"You mentioned a homeless guy before," I recalled, as I turned my attention to the ten-year-old with straight blonde hair. "What about him?"

"He looked nervous," the boy announced.

"Scared," another one said. "I've seen a homeless person before, with my parents. They always look sad, not scared."

"Anyone else?" I asked.

Several more hands went up.

"We saw a guy wearing a dark green jacket and dirty pants. He was by the big, steep lawn."

"Green Show Stage," one of the teachers translated.

"So, we have a homeless guy and someone wearing a dark green jacket," Vance said, as he made some notes in his notebook. "Did anyone catch what they looked like?"

"Brown hair."

The kids started to nod.

"Yes, brown hair."

"Which one?" I asked. "The homeless guy or the guy with the green jacket."

The kids stared at me as though I was speaking another language.

"What?"

"It's the same guy," one older boy said, shaking his head. "Duh."

"Woof."

About ready to crack a smile, and pat Sherlock on the head for coming to my defense, I noticed the little boy wasn't looking at me. Neither was Watson, for that matter. Vance and I hurriedly shared a look before turning to look back, at Sherlock. Both corgis were on their feet and staring at an empty spot on the wall, near a set of double doors. Confused, I stepped behind the dogs and checked for myself where they were looking.

"There's nothing there, guys. Sherlock? Watson? What is it?"

"Woof," Sherlock repeated.

"Ooooo," Watson howled.

I looked at the closest teacher. "What's on the other

side of that wall?"

The first teacher shrugged, but the second, Ms. Dodson, held out a hand. "Pass me that pamphlet, would you? Okay, we're here, and that way would be this direction, so … New Place, maybe?"

"A new place?" Vance repeated, puzzled. "There are probably many new places out there that we haven't seen. I'm not sure how that helps us."

"There's no *a*," Ms. Dodson clarified. "New Place. It's the name of William Shakespeare's home. I mean, it's obviously not the real thing, but it's a darn good reproduction of what his real house in Stratford-upon-Avon looks like."

Both Vance and I stared at the teacher in shock. There was a building here that was a recreation of the house that William Shakespeare once lived in?

I looked down at the dogs before Vance whipped out several business cards. He handed them to each teacher.

"You guys have been incredibly helpful. Stay in here as long as you can, okay? Call me when you're ready to leave. I'll make sure it's safe. Sherlock? Watson? Lead the way, guys. Kids? Stay in school!"

We hurried out of the amphitheater and followed the dogs as they pulled us to the left. There, just as Ms. Dodson had predicted, was a large five-gabled, three-bayed, half-timbered house. This *had* to be it.

"There's a sign next to the door," Vance quietly told me. "Yes, this is it! It reads, 'New Place, or Great House, home of William Shakespeare'. It says it's closed, even though this other sign says it should be open. Coincidence?"

The hair on Sherlock's back suddenly stood straight up. His lips peeled back and he let out a snarl. Watson scooted next to me and tried to get between my legs. What in the world was going on?

I saw that Vance was reaching for the door knob. I also noticed that Sherlock was on the verge of biting him. Then, it clicked: Sherlock was warning us about what was on the *other* side of the door.

Stepping forward, I laid a finger to my lips and then pointed at Sherlock. Then, I pointed at the house. Vance's eyes widened and his gun appeared in his hand. Motioning for me to stand back, he gently eased the door open. That's when we heard a low, sinister voice arguing with a woman's, and the poor lady sounded like she was sobbing. What's more, as soon as I heard the voice, I knew who it was.

"You w-w-will tell me wh-where it is, or s-so help m-me, I w-w-will k-k-kill you right h-here, r-right n-n-now!"

TEN

"But … I don't know anything!" the woman wailed. "I don't know what you're talking about. If you'll just tell me what you want, then I can help you find it! I swear! I'm not trying to hide anything!"

"It's m-missing!" the voice insisted. "Y-you've t-t-taken it for y-yourself!"

"I haven't!"

Vance cracked the door open and we both peered inside. A matronly lady, around my mother's age, had her back to us. She was in a floor-length dress, and judging from the straps we could see around her neck and her waist, was also wearing an apron. Perhaps this is what housekeepers wore in Shakespeare's time? As for the owner of stuttering voice, we couldn't see him, as he was just around the corner, out of eye-sight.

Just then, several books and a sheaf of papers sailed through the air, thrown—no doubt—by our desperate fugitive. The books crashed noisily to the floor, and in that brief time, Vance used the distraction to slip inside. Motioning for me and the dogs to stay outside the open door, he slowly advanced. Unfortunately, Tiny Dude chose that time to put in an appearance as he angrily stomped around the room, looking for whatever it was that was vexing him.

They both raised their guns at the same time.

"Detective Vance Samuelson, Pomme Valley police. Drop your weapon."

In the blink of an eye, Tiny Dude leapt for the lady he had been yelling at and held his gun to her head.

"No ch-chance. D-drop y-y-your gun, c-cop!"

"We've already got your accomplice," Vance smoothly returned. His gun, I should point out, never wavered as it tracked the fugitive from one end of the room to the other. "Give it up, pal. There's nowhere for you to go. Let the woman go. We can talk this out."

"Th-there's n-n-nothing t-t-talk 'b-b-bout!"

His stuttering was getting worse. That could only mean he was getting more and more agitated. We already knew he killed that Roseburg guard in cold blood. I could not let him do anything to Vance or the old woman. Coming to a decision, and hoping against hope that what I was going to do wouldn't exacerbate the situation, I knocked loudly on the door before strolling inside.

"Vance? Come on, dude. What's the holdup? Where are you?"

Tiny Dude yanked the woman with him as he twisted

in place to stare uncomprehendingly at me and the dogs. Seeing the gun, I hesitantly raised my hands.

"Oh, sorry. Am I interrupting something?"

"Wh-wh-who are y-y-you?"

"Oh, I'm just the guy who owns the dogs who've tracked you for a while now. I gotta let you know, pal, you're not an easy person to find."

I risked a glance at my friend, who was staring at me with a dumbstruck look on his face.

"H-how d-did you f-find me?"

I squatted next to the dogs. "This is Sherlock, and that is Watson. They're pretty good at solving crimes. They've solved murders, thefts, and missing person cases. They may not look it, but they're some of the smartest dogs I've owned. Oh, I'm sorry. Zack Anderson. And you are?"

"D-danny."

"Danny, do you have a last name?"

"N-n-no."

"It's okay, Danny. Listen, can I ask you a question?"

Danny shrugged. His grip on his weapon never faltered.

"What's the deal with the ham radio transmissions? In this day and age with modern cell phones, why resort to using something that's a little archaic when compared to cellular technology?"

"Kn-knew they'd b-b-be listenin'."

"Who? The police?"

Danny nodded. His stance, I'm happy to report, started to relax just a little. Vance, I could see, had partly relaxed his stance, too. Now that he knew I was getting our perp to talk, he kept quiet.

"So, the ham radios? Do you like using them over cell phones?"

"N-no. J-jake's f-fault. H-he uses th-them all the t-time. T-talked me into it. N-never sh-should've listened t-to the f-fool."

I pretended to think for a few minutes before nodding my head.

"Oh, I get it. You knew there were lots of people looking for you, so you and your accomplice must've decided if things went wrong, you'd switch to ham radio. Less likely someone will be listening, is that it?" I didn't understand his logic, since people all over the world could tune into the ham frequency, but hey, this wasn't the time to point that out to him.

Danny shrugged, which was probably the only affirmation we were going to get from him.

"Look, Danny," Vance said, as he slowly lowered his gun, "no one needs to get hurt here. See, I'm putting my gun away. We can talk this out."

Danny, however, showed no signs he was interested in lowering his weapon.

"Trust me, we want to end this situation as peacefully as we can."

"H-how did th-those d-dogs find m-me here?"

I shrugged. As nervous as I was, I was determined to try and keep a calm, neutral expression on my face at all times.

"I wish I could tell you. In fact, I wish someone would tell *me*. The only thing I can say is that these two are definitely smarter than you or I will ever be."

The briefest of smiles appeared on Danny's face before it quickly faded away.

"Wh-what's r-radio got t-to w-with it?"

Seeing an armchair nearby, I pointed at it and waited for

Danny to respond. Our armed assailant eventually nodded. Once I was seated, with both dogs' leashes wrapped tightly around my hand, I smiled yet again at Danny. I can honestly say I haven't forced a smile this many times since I was caught sneaking a soda at the movies, with Jillian.

"Thanks. The ham radio. That threw us for a loop. Turns out, another animal I have picked up on that. I came to own an African gray parrot. They're one of the most talkative birds out there. Well, this one loves to repeat anything she's heard. She heard your transmissions—the one about the virgins made me laugh, by the way—and gleefully repeated them to whoever would listen."

"B-birds can't p-pick up th-those m-messages," Danny argued.

I held up my hands in a *now just you wait* gesture. Pulling out my cell, I held it up, as if it was Exhibit A at a trial.

"Look. You're familiar with these, aren't you?"

Danny nodded.

"Okay. Now, look." I gave him the greatly simplified version of how I'd received their transmissions over my TV set and Ruby had picked it up. "I'm guessing your friend Jake Plinski couldn't put the pieces together?"

Danny's face darkened. "N-no. D-damn f-fool."

"You don't need to worry about him anymore," Vance said, adopting as friendly a tone as he could under the circumstances. "Mr. Plinski is in custody, and you'll be pleased to know he hasn't mentioned a single word about you."

While Vance was regaling Danny with what was in store for the former accomplice, I noticed I was still holding my cell. Dropping my arms to my sides, I carefully activated my Contacts app and there, on the display, was where I left off the last time I had used this application. What was on the screen? The contact information for Officer Stanley Ogden of the Roseburg police. I tapped the number and slid the phone into my pocket.

Danny, thankfully, didn't notice.

"Why Ashland?" Vance was asking. "Look at this place. It's small, when compared to Medford. Why not stay a little further north?"

"M-missed exit," Danny reported, sounding glum.

Vance sighed. "You missed your exit on the freeway, discovered you were here and didn't know what to do?"

Danny shrugged again. His face fell and he stared at the ground for a few moments. In the meantime, Vance looked over at me and held up his hands.

Keep him talking! I mouthed. *Stall!*

"What happened to you two?" Vance wanted to know. "How did you end up separating?"

Danny scowled and didn't say anything.

"You were tasked with hiding the money, weren't you?" I guessed. "You didn't want both of you to know the location, so you went one way, and he went the other, didn't he?"

Danny didn't say anything, but I could also tell he didn't have to.

"That's why you were sending ham radio messages," I continued. "You knew Jake would probably be listening, and you needed a way to tell him where to look without alerting the authorities. How am I doing?"

Danny refused to answer, nor was his gun lowered. I couldn't help but recall that this person was responsible for killing that guard in Roseburg. Regardless of how he acted, we couldn't let our guard down. And, seeing how Vance had yet to relax his stance, that meant he was prepared to act at a moment's notice.

"You did a good job hiding the cash," Vance admitted. "No one has any idea where it's hidden."

"That's why Jake was found wandering outside in Pomme Valley," I said, keeping my voice as emotionless and flat as possible. "He knew the clues referred to something outside, only he had the wrong city. I can't imagine what led him to believe it was PV and not Ashland. Because of that, he was found, and immediately incarcerated."

Vance nodded at Danny. "So, Danny, let me ask you something. What could have possibly happened that lured you here, out of hiding? Why risk exposing yourself in public when you know everyone in the state is looking for you?"

I was ready with my answer.

"Because, we were closing in on the location of the money ourselves. Danny needed to get it back before the authorities did. That meant he had to collect the money in person. Since Jake was only apprehended yesterday, Danny was bound to show in Ashland at any time. Looks like he beat all of us here."

With a cry of rage, Danny pressed the muzzle of his gun against his hostage's temple.

"It w-was in h-here, in th-this v-very r-room. Y-you t-t-tell m-m-me where you took it or s-s-so help m-m-me, I'll k-k-kill you right h-here, right n-n-now."

"But, I'm new here!" the woman wailed. "I have no idea what you're talking about! Just tell me what you're looking for, and m-maybe I can help you find it?"

"She has a good point," Vance pointed out, using a calm voice. But, I could also hear the tension rising with him, so I knew it'd only be a matter of time before one of them did something drastic. "What are you looking for, Danny? Zack and I have been all over this area earlier today. Maybe we saw it and didn't realize what it was?"

"N-no! Y-y-you're l-lying!"

I held up my hands. "Danny? Hey, look at me, okay? I don't want this to end badly. None of us do. You want the money from that bank in Roseburg? Well, we'd like you to have it, too. It means you'd be on your way and no one else would get hurt. Am I right?"

After a few moments, Danny reluctantly nodded.

"Perfect. Look, I told you my dogs are great at finding things. You clearly don't know where the loot has gone, and the three of us don't, either. What do you say we see if Sherlock and Watson can find it for you?"

"What are you doing?" Vance asked, growing angry. "We can't give him the money."

I looked my friend directly in the eyes. "Chet. Remember him?"

Vance let out a heavy sigh and nodded. He held out a hand, indicating we should proceed.

"Danny? Will you let us look? Let go of her and just stand over there, near the door. It doesn't look like there's another way out of here. You cover the door, so you know we can't do any funny business, and we'll start searching, okay?"

Danny waved the gun in a circle, thereby giving us permission to start the search. He stationed himself in front of the door and watched us look.

"What are we looking for?" I asked, as I stepped over discarded books, upended chairs, and stacks of parchment.

"A b-bag," Danny finally answered.

"A duffel bag?" Vance asked, as he held his hands a few

feet apart, suggesting the duffel was medium-sized.

"N-no. L-like th-this."

The fugitive held his hands up, but less than a foot apart. We were looking for something the size of a small purse?

"How in the world did you fit that much cash into a bag that small?" Vance wanted to know, genuinely curious.

Danny shrugged and shook his head. Apparently, we weren't deemed worthy enough to have that question answered.

I gave the leashes a gentle tug. "You heard him, guys. We're looking for a small bag the size of a purse, I guess. Let's see what's here, all right?"

For the next twenty minutes, I led the dogs over every square inch of New Place. Granted, this house was huge, but then again, many of the doors didn't work. I'm guessing the majority of the house was a façade and wasn't meant to be this thoroughly explored.

Neither corgi was interested in a single thing, whether still on the floor, or in its place on the wall, furniture, or table. I thought we might've finally found something when they made it to the desk, but after only a few seconds, Sherlock pulled away. So much for that idea.

Not knowing whether or not my cell might still be connected in my pocket, I decided not to draw any attention to it and to stall for as much time as possible. So, as we went through the house, and in a further attempt to keep Danny distracted, I started to straighten up the areas where we were searching. Seeing what we were doing, the elderly housekeeper flashed me a nervous smile.

"Where does this go?" I asked, as I righted a wooden chair.

"At that desk."

Placing the chair in front of the desk, and picking up a stack of papers that had been swept onto the floor, I ended up restoring some order to the recreation of William Shakespeare's personal writing desk. A quick glance under the desk revealed a small collection of things that must have been displayed on the surface: quill pens, phony stoppered bottles of ink, and a few acrylic literature holders.

Once the pamphlets had been returned to their holder, I noticed a third piece of acrylic, face-down. Righting it, I saw that it was a simple message, stating that, due to some unforeseen trauma, until further notice, *he* would be unavailable. Shrugging, the announcement joined the rest of the clutter on the desk.

"Sherlock? Watson? You've been awfully quiet, guys. Are you sure you don't want to jump in here anytime soon?"

Sherlock looked at me, shook his collar, and was about to sit when his ears perked up. He turned to me, cocked his head, then faced Danny.

"Woof!"

Vance arrived at my side. "Who barked? Sherlock?"

"Yes. Either he's woofing at *him* or else he thinks whatever we need is out there."

"Has he shown interest in anything in here?"

I pointed at the desk. "They only hesitated a second or two over there. But, before I could get my hopes up, they moved on."

"What's on the other side of that door?" Vance asked.

"That's the way we came in, isn't it? I think the amphitheater is that way, where all the classrooms are."

"F-fine," Danny grumbled. "Maybe th-that is wh-where they p-put it. Let's m-move."

Fervently hoping the kids were no longer out there, the four of us, including the housekeeper, followed Sherlock and Watson outside. Sure enough, the dogs pulled us straight back the way we came. As we opened the doors and stepped through, several things happened, all at once.

First off, the kids were still there, unfortunately. Some of them, anyway. That was because they were in the process of being ushered out as quickly as possible by at least a dozen different police officers. I recognized Officer Jones from PV, and a few from Medford. The policeman nearest to me had an Ashland patch on his arm. In collective silence, the cops stared at us. For several seconds, no one said a thing.

Thinking we were stalling for time, Danny angrily pushed his way by the housekeeper and shoved both Vance and me out in front of him and angrily looked around. Then, catching sight of who was staring back at him, he let out a cry of alarm, shoved the housekeeper away from him, and tried to flee. Turning on his heel, he sprinted for the door, intent on barricading himself inside, only to realize—too late—that the caretaker had swung the door closed.

Danny hit the door so hard that the glass in the windows shattered and he was thrown back, onto his rear. When he fell still, I realized the impact must have knocked him silly. His gun flew out of his hand and slid toward the kids. Officer Jones laid a restraining foot on it before it could slide too close to the children.

"Well, well," one of the policemen said. This one had sergeant stripes on his arm. "If this is the person who I think it is, then we've been looking for him. I have no idea how you were able to lure him here, with all of us present at the same time."

I pointed at the dogs. "I didn't. They did."

"Oh, my. Sherlock and Watson, isn't it?"

Two corgi derrieres wriggled with delight.

"I've always wanted to meet you two," the sergeant exclaimed. "Good job, boys."

"Watson is a girl," I pointed out.

"What?" the sergeant demanded. "Who would name such a pretty girl after a boy?"

I glared at Vance and held up a finger. "Zip it, pal. Sergeant? It went with Sherlock. Trust me, she doesn't complain."

"Uuuhhhhh."

We turned to see Danny struggling to rise from his position on the floor. However, complicating his efforts was the fact that both of his hands were now handcuffed behind his back.

"Hello there," the sergeant exclaimed, adopting a cheerful tone. "Danny, is it? We at the Medford PD are so very glad to meet you on an official basis."

Danny grunted once, but didn't say anything.

"I don't suppose you'd care to disclose the location of the missing Roseburg cash, would you?"

"G-g-g-go t-t-t-t-to …"

Poor Danny was stuttering so bad that he couldn't finish his sentence. I'm sure the kids, and the teachers, weren't complaining.

"How did you know to find us?" Vance asked, as he flashed his police badge. "No one called you."

"That's not quite true." I slid my phone out and checked the display. My call to Officer Ogden was still active. Tapping the speakerphone icon, I held the phone up. "Officer Stanley? Are you there?"

"I'm here, Mr. Anderson. You have no idea how glad I am you called. Based on everything I just heard, I believe we can call off the search for Plinski's accomplice, can we not?"

"His name is Danny," I said, "and yes, you can. Thanks for having my back, buddy."

"Thank *you* for allowing me to help. Stay safe, Mr. Anderson."

With the call terminated, I turned to Vance and grinned. "Hey, you were keeping him distracted. Why not take advantage of it?"

Vance turned his attention to the housekeeper. "Are you all right, ma'am?"

A look of righteous anger appeared on the matronly, wrinkled face.

"I'm fine, officer. I'm so very glad that ordeal is over. I had no idea what was making that unfortunate fellow so angry."

There was a commotion behind us. The cops were trying to lead Danny away, but he was resisting for all he was worth. However, there was a reason we'd nicknamed him Tiny Dude. The two cops escorting him simply hooked their arms under Danny's armpits and hoisted him in the air. Kicking and struggling, Chet's killer was finally led away.

"What a horrible man," the housekeeper was saying. "I don't think I've ever met the like before. Oh, I'm sorry. I'm Patricia Nesdore. You can call me Patty. I maintain New Place, only … oh my, it's such a mess right now. You, sir. What's your name?"

"Zack Anderson, ma'am. This is Sherlock, and that's

Watson. And over there? That's Vance Samuelson. We're from Pomme Valley."

"What was he looking for?" Patty asked. "I kept trying to get him to tell me, but he wouldn't do it."

"A bag holding $750,000 in cash," I answered.

"That would be a big bag," Patty decided. "I would have noticed something like that. Trust me when I say it wasn't there."

"He certainly thought so," Vance argued.

"Maybe he was confused?" Patty suggested.

A thought occurred, and just like that, I was smiling.

"No, Patty, he wasn't. Let me ask you something. What's gone, for unexpected maintenance?"

"I haven't a clue," Patty said, shaking her head. "I've only been volunteering here for a few months now."

"At the desk," I urged. "I placed some papers and a collection of pamphlets back in their holders. I also put an acrylic holder, one holding a full letter-sized sheet with an announcement, on the surface. Do you know the one I'm talking about?"

"Oh, that? It couldn't possibly be involved with this."

"What are we talking about?" Vance asked, curious.

"It's a life-sized wax figure of William Shakespeare," Patty proudly proclaimed. "He came to us all the way from Madame Tussauds, in London."

"There was a figure of William Shakespeare here?" Vance asked.

"Seated at the desk, yes."

"And what happened to him?" I wanted to know.

Both corgis, by the way, were staring at Patty, unblinking.

"Some children spilled a drink on Mr. Shakespeare, then in a fit of desperation, tried to remove the jerkin to hide what they did. So, the clothing is getting cleaned, and the jacket is getting repaired."

"How long ago was the figure removed from display?" I asked.

"About a week ago," Patty recalled. "He should be back soon."

Vance and I looked at each other and grinned.

"And where is he now?" I wanted to know.

"With a retired costume designer, why? There's nothing to worry about. She's a professional, and has worked on numerous films."

"Where does she live?" Vance asked.

"Didn't I say? She lives in Pomme Valley now."

"I'm very glad you weren't hurt, ma'am," Vance told her, as he hooked his arm through mine and headed for the door. "Zack, we have someplace to be, wouldn't you agree?"

"Nice rhyme, dude. You ought to be a poet."

"Shut up."

As the four of us hurried toward the parking lot, I suddenly felt the leashes go taut. Not wanting to clothesline either of the dogs, I slowed down and grunted loud enough where Vance turned around.

"What is it? Come on, pal. We have to get going!"

"Look at them," I urged, as I pointed at the corgis. "Something has grabbed their attention, and I think we owe it to them to see what it is."

"Fine. Where do they want to go?"

I pointed to the east. "That way. What lies in that direction? More theaters? Maybe a gift shop?"

We followed our pair of Clydesdales to the intersection of Main and Pioneer. Heading east, on Pioneer, took us farther away from the theater, and the hub of activity that had descended upon it. However, when the dogs finally drew to a stop, Vance and I looked at each other and whooped aloud.

We were looking at a Wells Fargo bank.

"He dropped it in a safety deposit box! Sherlock? Watson? Great job, you two!"

"Not really," I pointed out. "How are we supposed to know which one? If that's what Danny really did, then there's gotta be a key or something."

"Perhaps that's what he hid on the figure of William Shakespeare?" Vance suggested.

"It's a good theory," I admitted. "I just hope we're right. If we don't find a key on him, then we're back to square one, you realize that, don't you?"

"Have faith in your dogs," Vance said. "I trust them, and so should you. Come on. It's time to put this case to bed once and for all. We have the costume designer's name and address. We can be there in about twenty minutes."

"What if we're misreading this?" I asked, nearly ten minutes later. We were in Vance's sedan and speeding—as fast as the Olds would allow—back to Pomme Valley. "I keep thinking that, if there *was* something hidden on the wax figure, then it would have been discovered by now."

"Would it?" Vance challenged. "She's a costume designer, not a detective. So, you find a key. What do you do with it? Hold on to it, of course. That way, you can give it back to the people in charge of the figure."

"You're figuring if she finds the key, then she'll chalk it up to being an accident it was there, is that it?"

"It's how I'd react. Stop worrying, Zack. We've got this in the bag."

Not yet, we didn't. You'll see what I mean in just a little while.

ELEVEN

Didn't I tell you there was a link to Pomme Valley?"
Vance was saying, as we sped back there. "I knew it.
I just knew it! Why, I wouldn't be surprised if it turns out
the missing money has been in PV all this time."

"The clues led us to Ashland," I reminded my friend.
"If it wasn't for some unruly kids, then PV would have
never entered the picture."

Vance waved off my concerns. Getting off of I-5, we
transferred to Highway 238, which would lead us back to
Pomme Valley.

"It's there. It has to be there!"

"Don't get ahead of yourself, pal," I told him. "We still
don't know if we're even looking for a key. Yes, the dogs
zeroed in on Wells Fargo, but that doesn't mean we knew

what they were trying to tell us."

"I think I have it," Vance was saying, as he clearly continued to ignore my objections. "Care to hear it?"

"Go ahead," I said, as I sat back in my seat. "This ought to be good."

Ignoring my sarcasm, Vance nodded. "Oh, it is. Listen to this. Danny and Jake hold up the bank in Roseburg. Things go wrong and a guard is killed. Now they know they have to make good on their escape, seeing how the entire state of Oregon is going to be after them. With me?"

"Twists and turns abound, but I'm still managing to hold on," I reported.

"Right. So, they flee south, which leads them our way. Now, it's my theory that they stopped off in PV to stash the money, and ..."

"There's a problem with your theory," I interrupted.

"Please hold all questions until the end," Vance instructed. "Now, where was I? PV, right. They stop in PV, they hide the money in a safety deposit box, and then look for a place to stash the key."

"They didn't have enough time for that," I argued. "Ashland is too far out of the way for these two knuckleheads to visit first. You're telling me they had the forethought to hide the money in PV and then drive all the way to Ashland, so they could hide the key?"

"What do you think?" Vance challenged. We entered PV city limits and turned right on 5th Street.

"I say we hold off trying to figure out exactly what happened until we find the missing loot."

Vance shrugged and kept driving. Several blocks up, 5th angled right and became Pinetop Street. The house we were looking for was somewhere up ahead, on the left.

Once we were parked on the side of the street, and the four of us had exited the car, the door to the house opened. A friendly elderly lady, wearing a red and white floral print blouse, faded blue jeans, and white crocs, walked out onto her porch. I don't know what I was expecting to find when we met this retired costume designer, but the smiling, grandmotherly-type senior, who was silently watching us, wasn't on the list. I guess I was expecting our contact to be much younger and wearing tie-dyed clothes and maybe a pair of colored eyeglasses? I don't know.

"This must be the famous Sherlock and Watson I've heard so much about. Patricia called, from Ashland. She told me to expect some company."

Vance held up his identification. "Detective Vance Samuelson, PV police. You probably know my companions. This is Zack Anderson and yes, these two are Sherlock and Watson. We're here to talk to you about some work you're doing on a wax figure."

The short, elderly lady held out a hand. "Tessa Björnson. It's a pleasure to meet you. Is this really them? The corgis who just recently met the Queen of England?"

"That's them," I confirmed.

Tessa opened her door and stepped to the side. "Do come in. And you two …you cuties are free to jump up on any piece of furniture you like, do you hear?"

Sherlock and Watson strolled into the house as though they owned the place. They immediately veered toward the first room we could see, which was the living room. They went for the loveseat and simultaneously jumped up to claim a spot. Sighing, I followed the dogs, and Vance followed me. Once we were inside, and settled into our seats, I had to whistle. This was not the home of any senior citizen I had ever visited before.

Bolts of bright fabric, still rolled up on their cardboard tubes, were everywhere. The corner closest to me had no fewer than a dozen bolts of various shades—and styles—of green fabric. Some had rhinestones, others had lace patterns, and yet others were simply plain.

Dress mannequins were piled along the left of the room. Lined up before the window were two rows of five dummies each, and all of them were wearing some type of outfit. I saw a few evening gowns, one was a tuxedo, several had the exact same outfit, only in decreasing stages of disrepair. Looking over at our host, I pointed at the four mannequins all wearing the same clothes.

"For a movie?"

"They're for a project I'm auditioning for," Tessa explained.

"Aren't you supposed to be retired?" Vance asked, as he pulled his notebook from his interior pocket.

"Yes, well, I tried being retired," Tessa told us, with a warm smile.

"How'd that work out for you?" I asked.

"Not so well. Boredom is my demon. I'd rather not waste what's left of my life sitting in front of a television, thank you very much. I still have energy to work, and since I love what I do, I put out a few feelers. So, what can I do for you fine gents?"

A sharp bark, nowhere near as loud as when my dogs get ignored during introductions, caused us all to jump.

"A thousand apologies, my darling dears. My question encompassed the two of you, too. I am at your service."

"William Shakespeare," Vance began. "You know we came from Ashland. Is it true he's here?"

Tessa nodded. "A simple cleaning and patch-up. I'm told a group of school children took some liberties with England's most famous poet, and then tried to hide the mess to avoid getting into trouble. So, seeing how I'm the one who assembled his clothes, and then sewed them on him in the first place, they called me to see about either changing his clothes or else cleaning the ones he had on. That's when I discovered the damage, of course."

"To the clothes?" Vance guessed, as he continued to write.

"Yes. Oh, it was nothing serious. In fact, I should be done with him by the end of the day."

I raised a hand. "Can we ask where he is now?"

"Who, the wax figure?" Tessa nodded. "Of course. He's back there, in my workshop."

Shrugging, I turned to the dogs. "There's a rumor that a key of some sort might have been hidden on him."

"A key?" Tessa repeated, puzzled. "Somewhere on his person? Oh, do you mean, somewhere within his clothes? Does this have to do with that bank theft from last week?"

"In Roseburg, yes, ma'am."

"Well, I have most of the clothes off. I've had them cleaned, inside and out, and can safely say that I didn't find any type of key. In fact, I didn't find anything out of the ordinary."

"So much for that theory," I groaned.

Vance held up a hand. "Just a minute. Are the clothes nearby? Can we see them?"

Tessa nodded. "Of course. You won't find anything, of course, but you're welcome to look."

We followed the clothing designer deeper into her house. Not waiting to see if the dogs were following, we entered what I'm guessing was a family room, only Ms. Björnson had converted the large area into her workshop.

An eight-foot long folding table was directly in front of us. It had a huge assortment of buttons, clasps, brooches, and pins scattered across the surface. Another dozen of the mannequins were in here, too, with most of them outfitted in some fashion. I saw clothes that looked like they belonged to Indiana Jones, Crocodile Dundee, Captain Kirk, and at least a half dozen more fictitious characters.

Turning to Tessa, I gave her an appraising glance. "You get around, don't you?"

Tessa returned my smile. "Recognize any of them?"

I started pointing at various dummies. "Indiana Jones, a Star Trek member who'll inevitably die in that red uniform, Buckaroo Bonzai, and … hmm. This one is a toughie."

"Which one?" Vance asked.

I pointed out a mannequin wearing a cheerleader's outfit.

Tessa sat on a nearby stool and smiled at me.

"Come, now. If you can guess the others, then this one should be a piece of cake."

I circled around the mannequin. "Yellow cardigan, beige sweater, white skirt, white socks, and tennis shoes. I know I've seen this before."

Vance held up his hands. "You got me, pal."

It finally clicked.

"Goonies! This is Andi's costume."

Delighted, Tessa clapped her hands. "Well done, Mr. Anderson."

"Why would you have costumes from movies in your house?" Vance wanted to know.

"There's big demand for quality costumes," Tessa

informed us. She approached the Andi character's outfit and straightened the sleeves of the yellow cardigan sweater. "As it turns out, people love my work. Now, you're looking for William? Mr. Shakespeare is right over there, on that folding chair."

Vance and I burst out laughing. There was William Shakespeare, all right, but he was wearing a set of pale underclothes, like he'd been on the losing side of an unfortunate night of playing poker. Plus, he was seemingly staring at us as though we were someone who had just interrupted his game.

"Where are his clothes?" Vance asked.

"They're the pile on the table next to him," Tessa answered. "I take it you want to search them? Here, allow me."

For the next fifteen minutes, we watched Tessa slowly—and methodically—go through every nook and cranny of the pile of clothes. She held up each piece and explained what it was that she was searching. Doublet, trunks, jerkin, and hose. All were painstakingly examined.

There was nothing to find.

"Did you wash these in a regular washing machine?" I asked.

Vance suddenly looked up. "Good question, Zack."

"Yes, they were. If you're insinuating that this key might've fallen out, well, it's possible. However, I would have found it that day. And, unless you're accusing me of withholding evidence in what I assume is an active investigation, then you are mistaken."

Vance held up his hands. "No, Ms. Björnson, I'm not doing anything of the sort. Quite the opposite. You have been incredibly accommodating. We just have to make sure we've covered all the bases, so to speak."

"You're more than welcome to check my lint trap," Tessa said, with a smile.

"That won't be necessary," I assured her. "We are clearly mistaken in thinking there was something on Shakespeare's person."

"Are there any other clothes?" Vance asked. "Did he have anything changed in the last week?"

"Believe it or not, I have three different outfits for Mr. Shakespeare," Tessa began. "I usually change them out once a month. However, I put him in this outfit nearly two weeks ago. He has a little bit to go before he'll undergo his next change of clothes."

As I stood there, staring at the incredibly life-like figure of the most important playwright who had ever lived, a notion occurred. And, for the record, I hoped I was wrong.

"Umm, I have another possibility."

Vance turned to me. "Go ahead, pal."

"What if ... and, Ms. Björnson, this is no attack on you, so if I offend, I apologize, but what if, when this fellow was moved, the key fell out of his pocket? Is that a possibility?"

Vance and I both turned to Tessa, but the costume designer was already shaking her head.

"No offense taken, young man, because I'm not the one who moved him. It was a team of three people, with special training in moving wax figures, who were brought in to move William for me. Ordinarily, when I change his clothes, he doesn't have to be brought here. But, the powers that be decided now would be a good time to give him a checkup, too."

"I take it he passed," I guessed.

"Correct. There's nothing physically wrong with him. Only his clothes were soiled, and very partially torn. I've already mended them and am just waiting to put them back on."

The two of us both looked down at the dogs, who were stretched out on the floor, but watching Tessa with wide, unblinking eyes. Was that a coincidence or just a fluke?

"Sure, go ahead," Vance said, sounding glum. "I was thinking we'd might have to go speeding back to Ashland, but it doesn't look like that is gonna happen now."

Right about then, I noticed the corgis' behavior. Flashbacks to all the other cases I've been involved with flew through my mind. Why weren't the dogs ready to go? If there was nothing here that was going to help us, then they would have led us back to the door. Instead, what were they doing? Watching Ms. Björnson. That could only mean there was something here we were supposed to see!

"Tell us more about Elizabethan clothing," I said, stalling for time.

I felt a nudge on my shoulder.

"Zack? You all right?"

"Yeah, I'm fine. Ms. Björnson, please continue."

Unsure what the two of us were playing at, Tessa eyed us for a few moments before shrugging. She picked up the first piece of clothing from the pile. She spread it open and held it up.

"This is called a doublet. It's a long-sleeved, waist-high jacket. Note the color of this one."

"What about it?" Vance wanted to know.

"In Elizabethan clothing, coloring means everything. Well, that, and the choice of fabrics, too. The darker— or brighter—colors were reserved for those with a high status."

"What's the logic in that?" I wanted to know.

"Those colors are harder to make," Tessa explained. She held the fabric out to me. "Do you feel this? It's velvet, a common fabric for nobility and the upper class."

Both Vance and I nodded, as though we were back in class and were being lectured by a teacher. Then again, in a way, I guess we were.

"Over the doublet," Tessa continued, "most men typically wore a jerkin. Now, I don't have William wearing one, because he's inside, and since I wanted him to be realistic, I figure he'd take his jerkin off indoors."

"What is your definition of a jerkin?" I asked.

"It's not my definition," Tessa told me. "Wait a moment. I think I have … yes. Look over there. Do you see the red and white top over there, next to the mirror?"

"What, the shirt?" I asked.

"It looks like a shirt, but it's a jerkin. It's a short-sleeved, tight-fitting jacket that is designed to wear *over* the doublet."

"Sounds uncomfortable," I decided, with a shudder. Upon seeing Tessa's blank expression, I gave her a sheepish smile. "I get warm very easily."

"Mm-hmm. Now, for the trunks."

"Swimming trunks?" Vance asked.

Tessa shook her head. "No, you'd recognize them once you see them. Hmm, I don't see any on display. Well, never mind. Trunks are essentially puffy shorts."

Numerous images of silly, archaic figures wearing those frilly collars and puffy shorts came to mind. I couldn't help it. I ended up laughing out loud.

"Know what they are, do you?" Tessa challenged.

"I believe I've seen English nobility wear them," I said. "Ruffled collars and puffy shorts. It's probably one of the most recognizable images you have ever seen."

"Like Shakespeare would wear a set of those things," Vance scoffed.

Tessa snapped her fingers. "Of course! Why didn't I think about that? Willian *did* have a pair of these things. Look. Do you see these? I had him in a pair of black trunks."

"Wow, that's a distinct look," Vance observed. "I can't say it'd work for me."

"Dude, I'd pay some serious bucks to see that," I chuckled. "Then again, if I want a laugh, I can just look up the dancing detective on YouTube and watch you with your Peter Pan outfit on."

The look Vance gave me wasn't so friendly. But, before he could say anything, he noticed the dogs. At some point, they had risen to their feet and positioned themselves so that they were looking *away* from us.

"What are they doing?" Vance asked.

Squatting next to the dogs, I draped an arm around each of them. "What's up, guys? Is there something else you'd like us to see?"

Sherlock rose to his feet, turned to Watson to give her a nudge, and trotted back to the living room. Had the corgis decided it was finally time to go?

The answer to that was no. We returned to the living room, but this time, the dogs sat in front of what looked like a fancy TV tray. On it was a collection of items I couldn't identify.

"What are they looking at?" Vance wanted to know.

"You got me, pal. Looks like there's something there, but I have no idea what."

Tessa leaned around us to see what the dogs were checking out. "Ah, there's nothing important there. Just a few things that need to be returned."

Curiosity piqued, Vance approached the tray and studied the items. "Like what? And, who do they belong to?"

"Oh, that? They belong to William, of course. Your dogs have great noses. I can only assume that they were able to smell the wax? It has a very distinctive aroma."

I held up my hands in a time-out gesture. "Wait a minute. Those things came off of the wax William Shakespeare? Would you mind if we take a look?"

Tessa shrugged. "It's no problem. They're just a few accoutrements. Let's see. We have a black velvet flat hat, which could be worn by men or women, by the way. I have made several and am proud to say William has worn a few of them."

The dogs paid no interest, so I didn't bother with taking a picture.

"Next up, we have a worn, leather satchel. It …"

My head snapped up as I detected movement from the dogs. Both corgis had risen to their feet and were staring at the bag as though it was crammed with doggie biscuits. As Tessa rotated it this way and that in her hands, I saw something metallic flash on one of its sides.

"What is it?" Tessa asked.

I pointed at the bag. "What's that?"

Our host looked at the bag and shook her head. "I don't know what I'm looking for."

"That right there, on the side facing you … is it a piece of metal?"

"Oh, this? No, it's just the logo of the company who made this."

I leaned forward for a better look. What I saw had my

eyes widening with surprise.

"Coach? You're using a Coach bag on a wax figure?"

Tessa shrugged. "I reached out to see if they'd design me something, and they came up with this. They didn't even charge me for it, so the least I could do is use it. Why?"

I thought back to us standing before Wells Fargo, in Ashland, and an explanation suddenly fell into place. I looked at my detective friend and pointed at the bag.

"It's a Coach bag."

"Yep, I know. I heard you mention it before."

"No, Vance. Coach. As in, stagecoach? As in …?"

"Wells Fargo. I'll be a monkey's uncle. They were trying to tell us to look for the word *coach*, not the bank itself."

Sherlock grunted once and shook his collar. However, he didn't lose interest in the bag. At least, not yet.

"This bag," I began, "was William wearing it when those kids made a mess of his clothes?"

Tessa nodded. "The actual time it's on his person varies. Sometimes he wears it, and sometimes he doesn't. In this case, yes, he was wearing it last week."

I held out a hand. "May I see it?"

The bag was passed over. "Of course."

Unbuckling the clasp, and lifting the flap, both Vance and I peered inside the bag. I'd like to say there was a nice, shiny key inside, but I couldn't. What I *could* say was that there was a small, tarnished bronze key with a few numbers engraved on the head. Vance snapped on a latex glove and lifted out the key.

"Is that what this fuss is about?" Tessa exclaimed. "Heavens above, I had no idea that was in there. The bag was still clean, so I didn't bother with opening it. Guess I should have?"

"You did absolutely nothing wrong," I told Tessa. "It's been a pleasure. Now, if you'll excuse us, we need to see about returning some money to its rightful owners."

Vance nodded and headed for the door. Sherlock and Watson, I might add, were right on his heel.

Bidding farewell to the friendly costume designer, I hurried to catch up to Vance. He had already loaded the dogs and had his car idling by the time I slid into the passenger seat. He turned to me and held up his fist.

"Way to go, buddy! Woohoo!"

I hesitantly bumped my friend's fist with my own.

"You're forgetting one teensy tiny detail."

"Oh? What's that?"

"We have no idea what the key unlocks. Look at it. It's old and dingy. It could be a storage locker anywhere from here to Ashland, and *that* covers a lot of ground, I'm afraid."

Vance whipped out his cell and, still holding the key, snapped a few pics.

"I'll get this sent out. Hopefully, our boys in the lab will be able to figure this out."

As I sat in Vance's Oldsmobile, with him heading toward the station, I suddenly thought back to the corgi clues and realized only one set of pictures might provide an explanation. There were several references, so perhaps one of them might offer the solution? Could it be? Could it pertain to the location of where the bag of stolen cash was hidden?

"Make a right up here, at the next stop sign," I instructed.

Vance looked over at me. "What? Why? Do I need to

drop you off someplace?"

"Well, you could, but I figured you'd come along. After all, I'm kinda thinking you'd like to recover the bag of stolen money. Okay, now make a left."

Confused, my friend complied. After a few minutes, we pulled into the parking lot and Vance shut off his car. Leaning forward, so he could see through the windshield, he let out a grunt.

"You're kidding. Why are we here?"

Exiting the car, I lifted Sherlock and Watson down, who immediately headed for the entrance. Motioning for Vance to follow, we walked into the Post Office. Sherlock and Watson headed to the left, where the many rows of PO boxes were, only there were also nearly two dozen standard storage lockers.

"You're kidding," Vance started. "There's no way they ..."

He trailed off as both corgis sat in front of a large locker on the bottom row. Snapping another glove on, and gingerly holding the key up where we could both read the numbers, we could see that it was a match for the locker the corgis picked out.

"I think I owe you two a free-for-all at the pet store," Vance said, as he carefully knelt next to the locker and inserted the key. Taking a deep breath, he twisted.

We both heard the lock give out several clicks. The door was released, and when opened, revealed a large, green duffel. Vance pulled it out, unzipped it, and spread it open. There, in front of us, were stacks and stacks of uncirculated Benjamin Franklins.

Noticing that someone was approaching, Vance quickly zipped the bag closed and spun on his heel. There, in front of us, was the postmaster, one Willard Olson. He was in his early seventies, he was single, and he smelled *strongly* of Bengay. Two eyes glared suspiciously at my friend before shifting to me. The suspicion, thankfully, melted away. However, what replaced it was annoyance.

"Mr. Anderson. And here I thought you might have forgotten where we were."

Taken aback, I stared at the thin, frowning, septuagenarian and held up my hands. "I'm certain I have no idea what you're talking about, Mr. Olson. It's a nice day, isn't it? Now, if you'll excuse us, we'll be going."

Vance hefted the bag onto his shoulder and headed for the door. Much to my surprise, Willard beat me there.

"Not so fast, Mr. Anderson. I have yet to see your wonderful dogs at our club meetings."

"Club meetings?" Vance asked, confused.

"The NW Nippers," Willard explained. "I am the president of PV's only herding club. Mr. Anderson has enrolled his dogs, only I've yet to see a penny of their dues."

My eyebrows lifted. "Oh, is that all you need? Not to worry, Willard. I'll get the check in the mail. Now, I'm sorry to do this, but it's police business. We've got to get going. Er, 'bye now!"

Vance and I laughed like school boys once we were back in the car. True to his word, we made one final stop after pulling victoriously into the police station, and that was to Fur, Fins, and Feathers. Vance, I might add, spent a good thirty bucks on each of the dogs, getting them chew toys, pig ears, and the dreaded pizzle sticks. That jerk picked everything he knew the dogs loved, and that I hated.

Oh, well. This wasn't about me, but about the dogs.

Those two corgis have proven, yet again, that they continue to be smarter than us ungainly bipeds. But, that's all right. For now, we get to say that we safely closed yet another case.

It doesn't get any better than that.

EPILOGUE

"This is so huge, Zachary. Are you *sure* you're okay with this? After all, there's no going back once they get going."

Jillian and I, each holding a leash, were standing in front of the large warehouse I had added to the winery not that long ago. From this vantage point, we had a great view of Lentari Cellars. My winery spread out ... er, I mean, *our* winery was spread out over fifty acres, and from up here, we could see the vast majority of it. What it also afforded us was a perfect vantage point to watch what was about to happen.

Located several hundred feet away was the farmhouse I had lived in ever since stepping foot on Oregon soil. The first night I spent in there was also the first night that I had

Sherlock. It was also the location of the first date I had with Jillian, where I actually cooked for her, believe it or not. Now, it was about to be turned into rubble.

"Having second thoughts?" Jillian asked, as she slipped her arm through mine.

I stared at the farmhouse. Yes, there were lots of good memories there, but there were also some bad ones. Being held at gunpoint. Having intruders sneak onto the property in order to get at Jillian. Having a mouse scare the bejeezus out of me, in front of my friends.

I shook my head and caught the foreman's attention. Standing by the track of a very large bulldozer, the foreman looked at me and tipped his head. I held up a closed fist, with my thumb pointing up. I watched him nod and start giving orders. Within moments, the bulldozer roared to life and positioned itself this way and that, looking for the best angle to proceed. It reminded me of a snake and how it would try and find the best place to strike. A loader fired up, and then I saw several dump trucks move into position.

"I've been waiting for this day," I said, as I turned to my wife. Giving her a hug, I watched the west wall, where my breakfast nook used to be, topple forward. "This is going to be good for us."

Jillian wrapped her arms around my waist and hugged me close. "Absolutely, Zachary."

"Should we get going?"

"Hmm? But I thought … I thought you wanted to watch the house torn down?"

"Pssht. I don't care about that. But, if we are going to catch that showing, we need to get going. Great. Now I'm rhyming."

"What showing? Are we going to the movies?"

"Kinda. I thought since, all things considered, we've had Shakespeare dropped into our laps, that we'd catch one of his plays at the festival."

Jillian's cute mouth formed an O of surprise. "You don't care for Shakespeare."

"I don't, no," I admitted, "but I thought I'd give it a try. Come on, how bad could it be?"

"Do you remember reading *Moby Dick*?"

Surprised, I nodded. "Actually, yes. It wasn't an easy read, if that's what you're wondering."

"Watching Shakespeare is rather like that. It's like, you know what point they're trying to get across, only using old English, it takes longer to make the point. Do you understand?"

"Are you trying to warn me that I'm not going to like it?"

My lovely wife giggled. "Something like that. So, what are we going to see?"

"*Taming of the Shrew*, what else?"

Jillian smacked me on the arm. Hard.

Turning, the two of us walked around the large wine processing center until we reached the opposite side. One of my former interns, Kim, was there, watching Caden man the front counter of the small retail store located in the front of the building. Surprised someone was actually working in the tiny shop, I was about ready to head inside, to ask a question or two, when I noticed several people milling about.

"I didn't know there were customers in there," Jillian said.

"That makes two of us. Hmm, that means complete strangers could be visiting the property during business hours," I said, frowning. "I'm not sure I like that."

Jillian peered in the window. Kim noticed and gave her a friendly wave.

"Well, it looks like they've made a purchase. Several, in fact. You're not thinking of shutting down the shop, are you?"

"Hmm."

"Zachary, every good winery has an area where the general public can purchase a bottle or two of the winery's finest. You don't want to take that away from them, do you?"

"I guess not. I'm just thinking that … you know what? I think I might have solved the problem."

Jillian returned to my side. The dogs, hoping we were going for a walk, were at the end of their leashes and were looking east.

"Do you see how narrow that strip of land is, right there? The one that looks like an easement?"

"Yes. What about it?"

"I say we level it out, pave it, and turn it into a public access road. Our private road can remain gravel. Maybe we could put up some fencing along here, too."

"To help define what is private and what is public," Jillian added. "I like it. Provided that piece of land is something we can turn into a road."

"True. Then, we could …"

I trailed off as a series of shouts came from behind me. While not able to hear what was being said, one thing I did notice was that the heavy-duty construction vehicles were being shut off, one by one. As soon as they were all off, an eerie silence descended.

"This can't be good," I decided. "What, did they hit a power line?"

We hurried down to the house and saw the western side of the farmhouse was gone. The bulldozer had apparently done an admirable job, but once the huge machine had entered the house, intent on demolishing everything in its path, the cement foundation had cracked. Once the huge machine had backed out of the way, it was revealed, however, that the foundation hadn't just cracked, but a huge piece had fallen through, into who-knows-what below.

The foreman came up to us with an angry look on his face.

"Mr. Anderson? You never told us you had a concealed basement."

"That's because I didn't know," I argued. "I've lived in this house for several years. I had no idea that was there. What's in it?"

I looked at the jagged six-foot hole and tentatively approached. Both Jillian and the foreman snagged my arms and pulled me back.

"Not a chance, Mr. Anderson," the foreman declared. "We don't know how much of the foundation is unstable. Clearly, *something* is down there."

"Is there any way we could take a look?" Jillian asked.

The foreman thought for a few moments before turning to his crew.

"Charlie? Back that dozer out of the way. Davis? Hop in the loader. Spin her 'round and bring that arm over. Hmm, who's the lightest?"

As we watched the crew prepare to lower the scooping arm of a backhoe down, into the opening, I felt a tap on my shoulder.

"What do you think they're going to find?" Jillian whispered.

"I wish I knew," I said, shaking my head. "If there's

something creepy in there, well, you're probably going to be witness to either a grown man peeing himself or else fainting on the spot. I don't know if I want to know whether or not I've been sleeping on something that disturbing."

The arm lowered, with one of the younger guys perched in the backhoe's scoop. Gripping the arm tightly, the guy kept urging the operator to lower the scoop.

"A little lower. Just a little more. Hold on. Hey, can someone toss me a flashlight?"

One of the men tossed a small flashlight over. Once lit, the young crewman leaned down, as if to get a better look. An expression of amazement washed over his features.

"Don't even think about it," the foreman warned.

Too late. The young crewman hopped off the scoop and disappeared from sight.

"I don't like this," Jillian moaned.

"Nor do I," the foreman agreed. "Benjamin? Get your butt back up here. Now!"

The arm lifted, and Benjamin's head appeared. He had a strange look on his face, but then again, it could be because of what he was holding. Once clear of the hole, the arm swung toward us and deposited the crewman back onto terra firma.

"What do you got there?" the foreman asked.

A narrow, crusted oblong shape was presented. Measuring a few inches short of four feet, Benjamin held the item up, as though he had just found a jewel in the mud. When everyone stared at him as though he had lost his sanity, Benjamin jumped down, turned to the metal scoop on the bucket, and gave the object a few solid whacks.

"I think you guys need to call someone," the crewman said, as he dropped the object at our feet. "There's more of this down there."

A sword, completely rusted over, but unmistakable in appearance, lay before us. It was an American cavalry sword, the kind used in the Civil War.

Neither of us said a word. Sherlock and Watson? They inched forward to sniff the antique weapon. After a few moments, Sherlock lifted a paw and set it on the sword. The absurdity of the situation broke the ice and everyone started laughing. It would seem Sherlock was telling us he would be taking the case.

AUTHOR'S NOTE

I have a few disclaimers I need to throw out there, in case anyone has visited the places I just described. For starters, in Ashland which is, indeed, south of us, there actually *is* a Shakespearean festival, and quite a well-known one at that. At the festival, I make note of the replica of New Place, which is a reproduction of William Shakespeare's home. Now, I describe it as an incomplete structure, really nothing more than a façade. I have no idea if that's true. If it is, great. If not … sorry! Also, I mentioned William Shakespeare wore a period flat hat. I took liberties with that, and with his satchel. I scoured the internet, looking for some type of confirmation he carried a satchel. Sorry to say, I couldn't find proof anywhere, so I added it anyway. :)

As you have also noticed, I threw in a direct reference to what's in store for everyone's favorite corgi duo and their humans. I thought it'd be really cool to have a hidden chamber in the house and not know anything about it. That is, until demolition day arrives and its presence is revealed. Therefore, we're going to move right on to the Case of the Rusty Sword, as Zack and the gang try to figure out what a secret chamber is doing on his property, how long it's been there, and who arranged to hide it in that particular foundation.

What else? Well, up next for me is the continuation of my new fantasy series, Dragons of Andela. I have the next title slated to be released by the end of April. After that, I'll write CCF16, and then fans of Lentari will rejoice, because we're returning to the magical kingdom for a spell. After all, a certain someone has created quite a mess, and only Steve and Sarah, along with the newly retired king and queen, are left to figure out what happened. Blast from the Past (ToL#10) is just *waiting* to be written!

That's it for now. Stay safe, people.

J.
January, 2022

Zack and the dogs will be back
in their next adventure,
Case of the Rusty Sword (Corgi Case files #16)!

Meanwhile, catch up on the entire
Corgi Case Files Series
Available in e-book and paperback

If you enjoy Epic Fantasy,
check out Jeff's other series:
Pirates of Perz
Tales of Lentari
Bakkian Chronicles

Jeffrey M. Poole is a professional author living in Oregon with his wife, Giliane, and their Welsh corgi, Kinsey. He is the best-selling author of fantasy series Bakkian Chronicles, Tales of Lentari, and the mystery series Corgi Case Files.

Jeffrey's interests include astronomy, archaeology, archery, scuba diving, collecting movies, and tinkering with any electronic gadget he can get his hands on. Fans can follow Jeffrey online at his blog: www.AuthorJMPoole.com

CPSIA information can be obtained
at www.ICGtesting.com
Printed in the USA
BVHW071338150322
631522BV00006B/233